JANIE BOLITHO was born in Falmouth, Cornwall. She enjoyed a variety of careers – psychiatric nurse, debt collector, working for a tour operator, a book-maker's clerk – before becoming a full-time writer. She passed away in 2002.

SNAPPED IN CORNWALL

JANIE BOLITHO

Allison & Busby Limited
12 Fitzroy Mews
London W1T 6DW
allisonandbusby.com

First published in Great Britain in 1997.
This paperback edition published by Allison & Busby in 2015.

A CIP catalogue record for this book is available from
the British Library.

10 9 8 7 6 5 4 3 2 1

ISBN 978-0-7490-1769-9

Typeset in 11/16 pt Sabon by
Allison & Busby Ltd.

The paper used for this Allison & Busby publication
has been produced from trees that have been legally sourced
from well-managed and credibly certified forests.

Printed and bound by
CPI Group (UK) Ltd, Croydon, CR0 4YY

CHAPTER ONE

Life always seemed to catch Rose Trevelyan by surprise. She constantly told herself that now she had passed forty she might occasionally try to be a bit more organised: ever since her early twenties, when she wrongly considered herself to be a mature adult, nothing had gone to plan.

But no matter how prepared she had been, she could not have guessed at the consequences which arose out of a meeting later that day.

Another perfect day, she thought, as she gazed out of her window at the ever-changing view of which she could never tire. It was early but already the sun was rising higher in an unrelieved expanse of blue which held no traces of the thundery clouds which had rolled around the bay the day before. The much-needed rain had not come. The sea shimmered and already Rose could feel the heat building up.

She squeezed a grapefruit and drank the juice while she made coffee and one slice of toast which she took outside to the wrought-iron bench. The crumbs she gave to the house sparrows who had nested in a hole in the masonry in the side of her shed.

At nine thirty she loaded her equipment into the back of the Mini, a car small enough to negotiate the narrow and awkward angle of the drive, then headed down the hill.

Crossing Newlyn Bridge she slowed at the bus stop to offer a neighbour a lift. She received a shake of the head and a mouthed 'No, thanks'.

Penzance was busy, far busier than it had been for many seasons, which was good for local trade, including her own. Yet it was always a relief when the tourists had gone home and things reverted to normal.

On the dual carriageway Rose accelerated, noticing the slow response to her foot on the pedal. The car needed what her father called a 'blow-out'; a long run, he claimed, was good for the engine. It was also time she had the Mini serviced.

Her destination was Gwithian. Rose turned off at the roundabout in Hayle and silently repeated the directions she had been given by her client. Mrs Milton's house was off the beaten track, but easier to find than she had been led to believe.

As she turned in through the gate Rose saw that the

cultured voice she had heard on the telephone was well suited to the property. Both exuded power and money. Rose would have preferred to be photographing or painting the scenery but the bills had to be paid.

She parked to the side of the house; Mrs Milton would not want a rusting yellow Mini in the forefront of the photographs. Seagulls wheeled silently in the air currents as she walked the thirty or so yards to the front door and the occasional chirrup of a cricket was the only sound to break the otherwise perfect silence. Heat rose from the drive and melting tar sucked at the soles of Rose's espadrilles. Her cotton shirt was damp between the shoulders.

From here, the sea was no more than a distant sparkle. A few stunted trees, bent to the direction of winter gales, stood in the grounds. Beyond lay nothing but sand dunes, their grass-tipped peaks motionless. Rose's critical eye took in the building. It was two-storeyed, solid, built with local granite and pleasing to look at. But the hanging baskets and tubs spilling over with purple lobelia and pink and purple pelargoniums were too garish against their starker surroundings.

There had been no response to the slamming of the car door and all the windows were closed. Rose wondered if she had made a mistake with the date. She rapped the metal knocker loudly and waited.

A middle-aged woman in an apron opened the door. She had a grim expression and a no-nonsense demeanour which seemed to suggest she had better things to do than admit strangers. 'Yes?' She screwed up her eyes suspiciously.

'I'm Rose Trevelyan, the photographer. Mrs Milton's expecting me,' she said, wondering why she felt obliged to offer an explanation.

'You'd better come in then. Mrs Milton's in the lounge.' She opened a door to the right of the wide hall and, if she did not quite announce Rose's presence in the way of an eighteenth-century footman, it was the next best thing. The door was shut firmly as the woman left.

'Mrs Trevelyan, I'm very pleased to meet you. You were highly recommended.' Gabrielle Milton did not say by whom, she simply extended a hand adorned with four rings. Rose took it and realised that, from where she had been sitting, her client could not have failed to notice her arrival.

'Would you like some tea or coffee, or a cold drink, before you start?'

'Nothing, thanks, I'm fine.' Rose smiled. She did not want to waste time indulging in small talk. The sooner the job was done the sooner she could get on with the things she enjoyed. 'Would you like to tell me exactly what you want?'

'Of course.' Gabrielle Milton bent to pick up a long-haired cat which was curled on a settee. Rose watched her supple movements and tried to estimate the size of the price-tag which had once hung on the kaftan affair she was wearing. Mrs Milton obviously took great pains with her make-up and her hair, which was dark and coiled on top of her head. But she was not vain, Rose realised: no attempt had been made to disguise the grey strands above her ears. Surprisingly, her skin was pale and clear. Mrs Milton had not moved down here simply for the benefit of the sun.

'This is Dilys. Ridiculously named after my mother-in-law.' Gabrielle smiled self-mockingly and Rose was sorry she had refused the offer of a drink. She suspected she would enjoy the other woman's company. However, she guessed what was coming next. Pets were worse than children when it came to photographing them. 'I'd like her in the picture, if it's possible. On the terrace wall, I thought.'

'Of course.'

Outside, Rose set up her tripod, chose a wide-angle lens and adjusted the focus of her camera. 'OK, I'm ready. Put Phyllis where you'd like her.'

Gabrielle did so, stroking the soft fur and murmuring an endearment which seemed to work because the cat arched and stretched, then curled up in the sun. 'It's Dilys, actually.'

'Sorry.' Rose decided to take the shots head on, not a view she normally favoured but one which would achieve a good balance. To one side of the house were several palm trees of differing heights, to the other, slightly set back, was a creeper-covered outhouse. She used various exposures and half a roll of film: there had to be something there which would please her client. As the shutter clicked for the last time there was a slight movement. Dilys had disappeared.

Mrs Milton required a hundred and fifty copies for personalised Christmas cards, first having toyed with the idea of Rose sketching the house. She told Rose they had only been in Cornwall for seven months and thought it would be a way of letting their friends see where they lived – 'without actually having to invite them down.' Unlike the people Gabrielle was used to mixing with, Rose had struck her as calm, a soothing person to be with, one in whom you could confide. Her mistake, she realised, had been to fill her life with people to relieve the boredom and futility of her own life in the city but who, in turn, bored her further.

She would, she thought, as she opened her book later, like to talk to Rose Trevelyan, to have her as a friend.

But Gabrielle Milton never got the chance.

The small amount of air that was circulated through the open car windows was warm and offered no real relief. Rose was tempted to pull in at the first pub with a car park and treat herself to a lager and lime but decided against it. Procrastination had been her downfall on other occasions. She had, she realised, felt a little uneasy in Mrs Milton's company although there seemed no reason for it. She smiled, remembering David's words. 'You're more superstitious than the Cornish,' he had told her.

'You should know, you're one of them,' she had

replied, laughing, but flattered because it was another sign of acceptance into a part of mainland England which was like no other. The climate, the people and the way of life were more reminiscent of southern Europe.

The sky was no longer blue but white and hazy. Heat, shimmering above the road surface, made the tarmac appear to undulate, mirage-like. There were few pedestrians about; locals would be at work, and holiday-makers were already on the beaches enjoying two weeks of what Rose had all year round.

She did a mental calculation of outstanding jobs. If the weather remained hot she would work outside, leaving the developing of the Milton film until one evening because the darkroom was stifling in the daytime. Five new views were required for a postcard company for whom she worked freelance and Barry Rowe had asked when he could expect some new watercolours which he would reproduce for his greetings card firm. The photographic work paid the bills, but it was painting Rose loved. However, she had learnt early on that although she was good it was impossible to sell enough paintings to make real money.

Rose decided to take the car home. It was too hot and too busy to remain in it longer than was necessary. The Promenade was packed as couples and families enjoyed a light sea breeze, a breeze which now gently lifted the loose strands of hair around Rose's face and cooled her burning cheeks.

She parked in her driveway, facing the wall, on the

off-chance that it might rain later. The Mini was a bad starter when the engine was damp. Once the camera was unloaded and the gear back in its cupboard, Rose picked up a sketchpad and left again, on foot. The walk to Mousehole took just under half an hour and the road, at times without a pavement, held a continuous stream of traffic. Every visitor went there at some point of their holiday, delighted with the narrow rabbit warren of streets, none forbidden to traffic, which formed the ancient fishing village.

The local bus was making its complicated manoeuvre in order to be facing the right way for its return journey to Penzance. It was full, with passengers standing. Leaning against the harbour rails, the overflow from the pub stood with drinks in their hands. There was a smell of grilling fish as she passed the restaurant window.

On the far side of the village, and high above it, was a vantage point from which Rose had decided to sketch. Views of Mousehole and Newlyn were always popular but she tried to vary them as much as possible.

Absorbed in her work, she hardly noticed the time passing and only when she saw how far the sun had moved round did she decide to call it a day. Besides, she was thirsty, having forgotten to bring a flask, and her stomach told her it was time to eat.

Cars were crawling back along the road, their drivers slowing to admire the curve of Mount's Bay. They would return to hotels and guest houses to shower away the sand and salt before a drink and dinner. Rose, too, would do the same.

Laying the four sketches she had made on the kitchen table, she felt pleased with the results. Now complete with pastel watercolours they were just what Barry had said he wanted. It was one more job out of the way.

Rose let the jets of water run over her body for ten minutes, easing her joints, stiff from the long walk, then she washed her hair. Clad in a robe, with her head wrapped in a towel, she went downstairs to open the white wine she had put in the fridge that morning and which she sipped as she prepared a salad to go with a salmon steak.

Dennis Milton left his office carrying his suit jacket folded over one arm. As soon as he was in the street he jerked his tie to one side to loosen it and undid the top button of his shirt. London, in a heat wave, was unbearable. Gabrielle didn't know how lucky she was.

He made his way through the crowds in Regent Street and joined the throngs in Piccadilly. The traffic, at a standstill, allowed him to cross the road against the pedestrian lights. The air was filled with diesel fumes belching from buses and the sound of irate taxi drivers' horns. He turned the corner and found relative peace in the bar of the Duke of Norfolk.

Dennis was meeting a colleague with whom he was in the habit of having an early evening drink. He did not like to admit that since Gabrielle had become ensconced in Cornwall what used to be a couple of pints now usually developed into quite a session. At least he no longer had to rush home to change for one of the numerous social events his wife used to arrange. She seemed to have slowed down, he thought as he raised his hand in greeting, to be content with her own company.

'Usual, Dennis?'

He nodded.

Gordon Archer summoned the barman and asked for a pint of bitter. 'How's it going? Haven't seen much of Gabrielle lately. Isn't she coming up for a spot of shopping, or the theatre? I would've thought she missed being in town.'

'What?'

'Your wife, old son. Doesn't she miss the city? Mine would, I know that.'

'No. She loves it down there. She's taken up all sorts of new hobbies. Besides, I can take her any of life's luxuries she can't get locally.'

Gordon glanced at him quizzically. Had he detected a hint of vituperation in Dennis's tone? 'Anything the matter?'

'No, nothing. Difficult day, that's all.'

'Drink up then, we'll have another. This heat's getting to everyone.'

Dennis tried to smile and contribute to the conversation but he was worried. He had heard that his firm were after young blood, that those not coming up to scratch were to be given the elbow. It was silently implicit that target figures were not simply to be reached, but exceeded, if employees wished to retain their positions. They were only rumours, but rumours in the music business in which Dennis worked were usually founded on certainty. Of course, he had been with the firm long enough for there to be the offer of a substantial redundancy settlement – there was no question of his being dismissed – but it would mean living on Gabrielle's private income and he was not sure he could cope with that. At fifty it was unlikely he would get another job. Ageism, he thought, was more rife than any of the other isms but no one seemed to take up the cause. Probably because they're past it, he silently but cynically said to himself. The solution would be for him to move to Cornwall where they could survive on less money. The house was paid for – not by himself – and they could sell the London flat. At least he and Gabrielle had reached the point where they could survive a whole weekend without their discussions degenerating into a slanging match.

'My shout,' Dennis said, seeing Gordon's glass was empty. He took some keeping up with.

'I don't know how you do it, up and down every weekend. Is it worth it, all that travelling?'

'It is to me. The golf's good, the air's clean and the scenery is terrific. And there's the added advantage of mild winters.'

'I still say it's a hell of a way to go for it. Why not Surrey or Sussex like the rest of us?'

Dennis shrugged. He could hardly say that was precisely why it wasn't the south coast, nor did he explain how relaxed he was able to be once he had crossed the Tamar. Tired of Gordon's company and especially of the way he denigrated his wife, Dennis left early. No matter how annoyed with her, he would not dream of speaking to anyone about Gabrielle the way Gordon did about Helen.

He was still not used to the emptiness of the flat when he returned in the evenings. The large house in Wimbledon had been sold once their son, Paul, left home. It had always been too big but they used to entertain at home more in those days, instead of in restaurants, and they had wrongly assumed there would be more children. Gabrielle's sudden decision to buy a place in Cornwall had come as a complete surprise but Dennis could hardly tell her how to spend her money.

He missed her. Even when they argued she was company and now he saw less of her he realised that, paradoxically, he had enjoyed their rows, that life had never been dull. Certainly it was better than Maggie's farcical compliance. She was a fool if she thought he didn't see through her.

The cleaning lady had restocked the freezer but there was nothing which tempted him enough to bother to cook. Dennis poured a stiff drink and added a splash of soda, then sat down, resting his head against the back of the leather settee, welcoming its coolness. He put his involvement with Maggie down to what people chose to call the male menopause and now he was sorry he had let it go on so long. Maggie was sending out messages he did not want to receive and he was not sure how to end the relationship. She was single and independent and, initially, she had been fun to be with, but Dennis felt he was being drawn into a trap. Maggie, he sensed, would very much like to replace Gabrielle.

The telephone rang and his hand holding the drink jerked. He had been on the point of falling asleep. Another bad sign: too much booze and not enough food.

'Hello, darling. I'm surprised to catch you in.'

'Gabrielle.'

'Are you all right?'

'Fine. You?'

'Yes. Look, I thought I'd better let you know I've organised the Christmas cards from this end. Tell Fiona, or she'll go to the usual people.'

Christmas cards? Christmas was four months away. But Gabrielle was right, his secretary Fiona took rather too much upon herself, to the extent once of buying a silver and crystal rose bowl she thought suitable for his wife's birthday present. Dennis would not have chosen it himself but felt obliged to reimburse her. If he was given the push, would Fiona be out of a job as well? Gabrielle was telling him something about some photographer she had commissioned.

'How much is that little lot going to set us back?'

'No more than if you get the usual printers to do them.

It's not like you to question me over money, Dennis. I don't waste it, you know that.'

'I know. I'm sorry. I'll ring you tomorrow. Take care.' Dennis replaced the receiver. Tomorrow was Thursday and he had agreed to take Maggie out. Perhaps he ought to ring her now and cancel. Surely she'd get the message if he did it often enough.

Then Friday. How he looked forward to it these days. Gordon was wrong, he loved the four and a half hour journey, relaxing on the train with a drink and a sandwich, the evening paper and a book. It was a kind of no-man's-land, between the city and work and the slow, easygoing atmosphere of Cornwall. He had a regular booking on the Golden Hind from Paddington which reached Redruth just after ten. Gabrielle met him in the car – Dennis had no need of one in London – and dropped him back for the first train on Monday morning.

He would, he decided, make it up to her this weekend, take her out somewhere special, maybe, instead of playing golf.

With a wedge of Stilton and a couple of crisp breads serving as his evening meal he poured one more drink and took it with him to bed.

CHAPTER TWO

Eileen Penrose and her sister, Maureen, were sorting piles of clothing and bric-à-brac into appropriate groups ready for the church jumble sale on Saturday. It was a task they had once taken on several years previously and it had become expected of them that they would continue with it each year.

'Just look at this,' Maureen said, holding up a dirty shirt between thumb and forefinger. 'It's only fit for the bin. I'd be ashamed to send it.'

Eileen sniffed disdainfully and pushed her limp dark hair back off her face with a thin hand.

'Still,' Maureen continued, used to her sister's uncommunicative ways, 'Mrs Milton did us proud. I knew we'd get some good stuff from her.'

'Ah, yes. The lady of the manor.'

'Come on, Eileen, it's all in a good cause. Besides, you

don't object when she asks you to help out, you said yourself she pays generously.'

Eileen sniffed again and folded some sweaters roughly. The church hall was musty and smelt of old clothes. Motes of dust danced in the wedge of sunlight shining through the open door, but at least the building was cool. Eileen had no wish to discuss Gabrielle Milton.

'Look at this top, we'll get at least two pounds for it.' Maureen put the knitted garment with its leather appliqué work on a hanger where it would be more prominent. 'I don't know what you've got against her, she's quite nice really. Well, you should know that better than me, you see more of her.'

Eileen's face had reddened. Maureen decided to drop the subject because she knew exactly what her sister's problem was.

Eileen Penrose's husband, Jim, was dark-haired and handsome and his deep brown eyes hinted at seduction. Women were easy in his company; he teased them and made them laugh and they enjoyed the mild but meaningless flirtation. He was not unfaithful to Eileen, partly by choice but also because if he so much as propositioned another woman it would be all over the village before she had time to answer. Eileen had lived there all her life and must have known it, yet she carried her jealousy almost to the point of obsession.

In early February, not long after the Miltons had moved in, Jim had been called out in his capacity as a heating engineer to make some adjustments to the central heating boiler. 'You should see what they've done to the place,' he told Eileen after that visit, 'it's terrific. Wood block hall and carpets up to your knees.'

'What's she like?' Eileen wanted to know, interested only in the woman, not her possessions.

'She's a looker, I'll say that for her. She could be on the telly.'

That was enough for Eileen Penrose and when Mrs Milton rang a second time her lips were compressed with rage as she handed the telephone to Jim.

Both Maureen and Jim had tried to reason with her, to explain that Mrs Milton's needs were genuine. No work had been done on the heating system since it had been installed by the previous owners and several of the radiators were leaking where the joints had rusted. Maureen realised she would be wasting her breath explaining to her sister that women like Gabrielle Milton would not be interested in the likes of Jim Penrose.

'She's having a party, some sort of big posh do.'

Maureen waited, smiling to herself, knowing how the game was played. If she asked any questions Eileen would clam up.

'A week Saturday. All her London cronies, I suppose. She's asked me to help out,' Eileen volunteered.

'What about Doreen?'

'Oh, she'll be there as well. One of us to serve drinks, the other to see to the food. Finger buffet, she calls it. Whatever that might mean.'

'It's a few extra pounds in your pocket.' Maureen was

unable to understand how Eileen could work for, and take money from, someone she so obviously despised. Maybe it was a way of keeping an eye on Gabrielle. She shrugged and glanced at her watch. 'Come on, that'll do for today. I could do with some fresh air.'

Maureen locked the door and pocketed the key and told Eileen she'd pick her up at nine on Saturday morning when they could finish the last few bits.

The salad was ready, the salmon brushed with oil ready to go under the grill. As Rose waited for the new potatoes to boil she was surprised to notice she was already halfway down the bottle of wine. She had better take it more slowly. The condensation on the bottle was no longer a mist but had gathered in droplets and run down the sides leaving a wet circle on the kitchen table.

It's the weather, she excused herself, although she was aware that it was more than that and that she was desperately trying to keep other thoughts at bay. The kitchen was stuffy with the heat from the cooker. She lowered the gas and took her drink outside. She felt the warmth retained in the metal bench through the fabric of her skirt.

People shouldn't die in the summer, she thought, it doesn't seem right.

But her thoughts were really more specific. She meant David, David whom she had wanted never to die at all. It was four years now yet the pain was not far from the surface. She missed him more than she imagined possible even though she had had months in which to prepare herself. There were still times when she expected him to walk through the door; when suddenly in the street she thought she heard his voice; when she would say to herself, I must tell David that. Tall, easy-going and loving, he had died in the prime of his life, wiped out as if he was of no consequence. The anniversary of his death was in two weeks' time.

Rose pushed her hair behind her ears, dry now after her shower. She felt a tightening around her skull, the beginning of a headache caused possibly by the wine, but hopefully, by the way the clouds were banking up, by an impending storm. There was a sulphurous yellow glow in the distance.

Recognising her mood and knowing the danger signs, she had two alternatives: work or ringing Laura. She opted for work, but first she must eat.

The wine was returned to the space for bottles in the fridge; she might finish it later. A brilliant flash of blue-white light illuminated the kitchen, followed by a loud bang. Within seconds the sky darkened further; rain hammered on the windows and bounced off the bonnet of the car. Rose took herself up to the attic which served as a darkroom and developed Mrs Milton's film.

Engrossed in what she was doing she took several seconds to realise the telephone was ringing and she had not set the answering machine. With the film drying it was safe to switch on the light. She wiped her hands and went downstairs.

'Mrs Trevelyan? I'm sorry to bother you in the evening, but I was wondering if you'd like to come over a week on Saturday. We're having a bit of a do. Family and a couple of friends from London, but really it's for the people I've met down here. I know we hardly know one another, but, well . . .' Her voice trailed off.

Rose immediately guessed that the invitation was issued out of loneliness and not because a last-minute replacement was required.

'Thank you. I'd love to come,' she heard herself replying before she had given herself a chance to think about it. 'What time?'

'Any time after eight. I'll look forward to seeing you. Oh, I'll see you before that, won't I? With the proofs. No, wait, bring them with you, Dennis can have a say in the choice then and it'll save you a journey.'

Rose agreed to do so, then hung up. A party. She had not been to one since David died – and what would she wear? When did she last buy herself something new? And whom could she take? Gabrielle had said to bring a guest if she wished. Rose shook her head. Ridiculous, she felt like a teenager going on a first date. Barry Rowe. She'd ask him. There was, she realised, no other male who came to mind.

Once she had cleared up in the darkroom, Rose poured out some more wine and dialled his number. Barry made no pretence of checking a diary or hesitating. He had known Rose since she first came to Cornwall and did his best to sell her work. Since David's death he had been her only escort. He had always hoped to become more than that but there seemed to be no romantic attachment on Rose's side. At least they shared similar tastes and found a sort of comfort in each other's company.

'I'd be delighted,' Barry told her. 'God, it's not evening dress or anything, is it?'

Rose laughed. 'No, Gabrielle said it's informal.' Although that still left her in some doubt as to what would be suitable attire. What the invitation had done was to take her mind temporarily off the looming anniversary. She finished the conversation by promising to bring in the watercolours she had completed.

Depressing the bar, Rose waited for the dialling tone, then rang Laura. 'Guess what?' she said. 'I've been asked to a party.'

'Oh? Anyone I know?'

'A lady called Gabrielle Milton.' Rose waited. Laura, born and bred in Newlyn, knew everyone, and the gossip surrounding them, for a ten-mile radius.

'Milton?'

'Mm. She lives near Gwithian.'

'Must be a newcomer.'

'Relatively.' Rose smiled. 'Anyway, I'm taking Barry.'

'Ah, the ever faithful Barry Rowe. Rose, why don't you go on your own? New people, new friends, you might . . .' Laura stopped, suddenly remembering the date and how tactless she would sound if she suggested it was an opportunity to meet a new man. 'Well, buy something exotic and have a great time. And if you need a chat, I'm always here.'

'I know. Thanks.' Rose did know. Laura had been the one to get her through the bad times after David died. 'Why don't you come up for a meal? Tomorrow? If Trevor's not home.'

'Great. I'll bring the hooch.'

Rose hung up. She had a nagging feeling of guilt but realised David would not mind the fact that she had something to look forward to. It was selfishly gratifying to Rose that Laura's husband was a fisherman, away for days on end. It meant Laura, unlike some women, had evenings free which they could spend together without worrying about being late or having a meal on the table. Her solitude, Rose realised, had changed her.

It was a mystery how her and David's lives had meshed so well. He was a mining engineer, methodical and tidy in all he did. Rose was scatterbrained and messy. Over the years they had had together they had adopted some of each other's ways until a middle path was formed. And David, forward-looking in all things, had been adequately insured. The mortgage was paid up upon his death; she had a small pension and her own business was gradually building up, now she was putting more effort into it. Rose supposed she had treated it more like a hobby until necessity deemed it otherwise.

Could she, she wondered, spare half a day to go into Truro to find something to wear? It would probably be worthwhile. Her wardrobe consisted of jeans and casual clothes, her manner of dressing a remnant from her student days, encouraged by the informality of her surroundings. Her hair, still shoulder-length and straight, either flowed loosely or, more latterly, in deference to the passing years, was tied back or twisted and held in place with a toothed, sprung clip.

It was still too early to go to bed. Restless, the storm noisily making its presence known, and her anticipation mixed with sadness, Rose put on some classical music. It usually soothed her, allowing her thoughts to drift. Leaning back in the shabby chintz armchair she closed her eyes. Sometimes it seemed like yesterday she had stepped off the train at Penzance station and begun walking to the lodgings her parents had insisted she booked before she set off. Resting against the rails near the open-air swimming pool she had understood why artists flocked to the area. The colours of both sea and sky were unbelievable and she knew she would feel at home.

Her parents had financed her for six months after she had finished college. When the money ran out she started painting in earnest. She did not want to leave.

Barry Rowe came into her life soon after. Rose had gone into the shop from which he sold the cards his small firm produced and asked if he would be interested in any of her work. He had liked it and said so. On a future visit she met David. He was looking for a birthday card and happened to choose one which Rose had originally painted.

'The artist's standing behind you,' Barry Rowe had said, grinning.

'Oh?' David had turned around and something passed between them. Rose could never recall exactly how it was that they ended up having a pub lunch – one of them must have started a conversation. A year later they were married.

Rose opened her eyes. The wind had dropped, apart from the occasional squally gust, and the rain had eased, or ceased altogether. Her neck was stiff and the music had finished. Glancing at the small carriage clock on the low stone mantelpiece she was amazed to see that it was two thirty. It was the best and deepest sleep she had had for some time.

Maggie Anderson chewed the corner of her mouth in frustration. It was the third time Dennis had let her down recently. His excuse was pressure of work but she knew by his tone he was lying. Gabrielle was safely out of the way, there was nothing to fear as long as they avoided places where Dennis was known. He refused to take her to the flat – which, she supposed, was understandable. His wife had chosen and furnished it and had lived there with him. But Maggie hoped she wasn't losing her hold over him.

Ten years younger than Gabrielle and her opposite in looks and temperament, she believed she was exactly what Dennis needed, especially if he was to stay at the top. A suitable partner was an advantage: a partner who was attractive and witty and fun, yet knew where to draw the line. One who enjoyed socialising, something Gabrielle seemed to have given up. It was unfair on Dennis to expect him to attend functions and entertain clients on his own. Once or twice she had partnered him, introduced as a colleague. She knew enough about the trade to be able to converse knowledgeably albeit not in depth.

She stood in front of the mirrored wardrobe in her bedroom, dressed ready to go out. Dennis had left it very late to cancel. Tomorrow he would be off to Cornwall again. Maggie was fed up with weekends spent alone. He had mentioned the party, only, she guessed, because he was surprised at Gabrielle initiating it. That was the following weekend. Maggie smiled at her reflection, satisfied with what she saw. 'Why not?' she said aloud. 'Indeed, why not?'

'Oh, Rose, it's just *you*,' Laura said when she arrived, breathless from hurrying up the hill in the warm evening air. The storm of the previous night had only provided temporary relief. 'Here.' She placed some wine which had been in her woven bag on the table as was their custom when they ate in one another's houses.

'Do you think it's dressy enough?' Rose held the outfit in front of her and looked at it doubtfully. 'Yes. No one goes mad these days.'

The skirt was of pastel swirls, chiffon over a silky underskirt, the long, loose matching top of chiffon only.

Beneath it she would wear a pale blue silk vest the same colour as in the pattern. 'I suppose if I put my hair up?'

'Rose, you'll look lovely. I wish you'd stop worrying. Where've you hidden the corkscrew this time?' Laura had pulled open a couple of drawers, knowing things could not usually be found in the same place twice. Discovering it beside the bread bin she yanked out the cork, holding the bottle inelegantly between her knees. 'What shoes are you wearing? Don't tell me, you forgot. You can borrow my white sandals, I've only worn them twice.'

'Thanks, Laura.'

The same size feet was all they had in common physically. Laura was several inches taller than Rose, and thinner, her hair cut level with her ears, the dark curls awry. Laura hated her hair but Rose always pointed out that people paid a lot of money to have theirs done that way.

Wineglasses at hand, they settled down for an evening of serious conversation and gossip, and, in an hour's time, some food.

CHAPTER THREE

The weekend had passed unnoticed. That is, for Rose, the days were the same as any other. She took advantage of the weather and continued with outdoor work apart from a quick job in Penzance on Saturday morning. The mother of a boy about to start secondary school wanted a professional photograph of him in his new school uniform. 'Before he ruins it,' she had added with a resigned expression.

Barry took her to the cinema on Sunday evening but they parted immediately afterwards. Then, with the weekend behind her, Rose found the rest of the week slipping by. She gave the following Saturday afternoon up to pampering herself: a bath, instead of a shower, and a coat of pale gloss on her fingernails. Her hands, she realised, could have been better taken care of but, despite rubber gloves, photographic chemicals had taken their toll.

At eight fifteen there was a toot from the main road. Rose did not recognise the car. Peering harder she saw Barry getting into the back seat.

Picking up her handbag she went to join him. 'A taxi?'

'No.' The driver laughed. 'Barry here's conned me into driving you over. You'll be coming back in a taxi, though.'

Rose turned and raised her eyebrows.

'Sorry. This is Geoff, works on the printing side.'

'Ah.' And probably Geoff had been responsible for printing the rather formal greeting in Gabrielle's Christmas cards. She had remembered to bring the proofs with her. 'Hello. Nice to meet you at last.'

'You, too.' Geoff smiled into the rear-view mirror.

The printing was done in Redruth but Barry had suggested Geoff make himself useful by collecting some urgent artwork and, whilst he was at it, dropping them off on his way home.

'Nice bloke,' Rose commented as they walked up the drive.

'Yes. Nice house.' Barry nodded towards the granite building, the stone softened by the warm tones of the sun as it began to set. There would be few more evenings such as this one. Of course, Rose remembered – it was the bank holiday weekend. How on earth could she have forgotten with the Newlyn Fish Festival on Monday?

The same woman Rose had seen before answered the door. She was wearing a brown dress, like something out of *Rebecca*, Rose thought, guessing it was the woman's own choice, not Gabrielle's. The look she received was fractionally more pleasant than on her previous visit. They were shown into the long lounge which ran the length of the house and which had once been two rooms.

'My, my,' Barry whispered, holding her elbow.

Gabrielle had decorated the room with flower arrangements; their scent filled the air. In the alcove in the far corner a table had been set up, covered with a cloth and holding an array of bottles and mixers. There was also wine but, to Barry's disappointment, he could not see any beer.

Rose was more interested in the other guests, one or two of whom she already knew and smiled at. She studied them not as people, but as subjects to paint. However, portraits were her weak area; she was never able to capture the essence of a character in oils.

'Mrs Trevelyan, I am so pleased you could come. May I call you Rose?'

'Of course. This is Barry Rowe.' Rose briefly explained what he did. 'I know one or two people here.'

'I'm glad. I'll introduce you to my family. Dennis?' She turned to address a tall, suave man in a yellow polo shirt and cream trousers. The man approached, smiling urbanely, obviously used to social gatherings. He also had the advantage of being on home ground.

Rose realised two things: she was slightly nervous, and she had allowed herself to get into a rut. As they were introduced, she hoped Barry did not feel out of place in a jacket and tie: no other male seemed to be wearing one.

'Ah, the photographer.' Dennis shook her hand. 'And I believe I'm to inspect your handiwork this evening.'

'Yes. The proofs at any rate.'

'Dennis, I'm sure our guests would like a drink first.'

'Of course. Over there.' He indicated the table, behind which a thin, scowling woman was pouring drinks. 'I don't think there's anything my wife's not got in.'

Was he, Rose wondered, being snide? Dennis had one of those impassive faces upon which emotions did not register.

'I don't see any food,' Barry said as they crossed the room.

'There's bound to be. It's probably in another room. Gabrielle won't want smoked salmon trodden into the Wilton.'

Rose asked for a glass of dry white wine with a splash of soda. If it was going to be a long evening she didn't want to drink too much. Barry took a chance and asked if there was any beer.

'What kind?' the woman said. Behind her were several crates of bottles, but, more importantly, a firkin of Hicks. His eyes lit up.

Glasses in hand they found Gabrielle at their elbow once more. 'I'd like you to meet my son, Paul. And his fiancée.' She led them to where the couple stood. Paul was undoubtedly his father's son. The girl with him was beautiful, her looks spoilt at that moment by the sullen downturn of her mouth. They were in the middle of some sort of argument and were only just polite. 'We might as well have a look at those photos now,' Gabrielle said, more to cover her embarrassment at her son's behaviour than out of real interest.

They went to a small room across the hallway and Rose laid them on a table. It was left to Dennis to decide; Gabrielle liked them all. 'May I leave them here until later?' Rose asked, not wishing to be left holding the envelope all night.

'Of course. They'll be quite safe. Come on, I'll let you get to know the others.'

Mike and Barbara Phillips were just arriving. 'Rose. Good to see you, and you too, Barry.'

'You know Dr Phillips?' Gabrielle seemed surprised, unused yet to the fact that it was a close-knit community.

'We're old friends, actually. Hello, Barbara, you look great.' Rose did not add that Mike had been responsible for David's hospital treatment and that it was he who had broken the news of the prognosis to her.

Guilt rose anew. What would Mike and Barbara think of her partying so near the anniversary of his death? And she wished Barry would not keep taking her arm in that proprietorial way. 'Excuse me, I need to find the toilet.'

'David,' she said, pressing her face against the coolness of the mirror. 'Oh, why aren't *you* here with me?' She stayed several minutes until she felt able to face the assembled company and make the required small talk. It had been a mistake to come.

There was no sign of Gabrielle but she made an effort to talk to strangers rather than huddle with people she knew. Barry, it seemed, was doing the same. Perhaps he sensed her earlier resentment.

'Doreen tells me the food's ready,' Dennis said, trying to make these new friends of his wife's at home although he barely knew anyone himself. There were two couples from London, real friends, not just acquaintances.

And Maggie.

And how he was coping with her presence was beyond him. Gabrielle seemed to have accepted that she was a work colleague Dennis had invited but who had had doubts as to whether she would be able to make it. Now was not the time to sort that little problem out. As soon as he was back in London he would make it clear to Maggie that the relationship was no longer viable. It had taken this semi-separation for him to realise how much he thought of his wife.

But where was she? Surely she should be presiding over the food? He grinned ruefully. If Doreen Clarke allowed it, he amended.

Most of the guests had already had several drinks and needed a base on which to soak up any more.

'Impressive,' Rose said quietly as she and Barry surveyed the trestle tables laid up on the patio at the back, the food protected by awnings which, when rolled back, were virtually invisible in their holders neatly slotted into the stonework.

'This is very nice,' Doreen commented.

'Oh. I'll try some then.' Rose gave Doreen the full benefit of her smile. The ice had been broken. 'Delicious. Did you make them?'

'Yes. It's easy though.' Doreen Clarke spoke sharply to disguise her pleasure. 'Mrs Milton and I did it all between us. She likes cooking.'

It was not easy to picture their elegant hostess up to her elbows in flour.

Barry remained silent, his mouth too full to speak. His plate, Rose noted, was piled high. She had never known anyone able to eat as much and remain so lean. Rose strolled across the grass. Paul and his young lady were nowhere in sight. Presumably they were too upset to eat. It was difficult conducting a row in a room full of people. She and David had done so once, hissing at each other out of the sides of their mouths. And the woman on her own, who was she? They had not been introduced, but Rose had noticed the grim glances Dennis Milton was throwing in her direction. Was there something not quite right going on there? Gabrielle didn't seem put out. Another one who wasn't hungry, Rose decided. Perhaps the sight of all that food as it was being prepared had put her off.

Relieved to see Barry in deep conversation with Barbara Phillips, Rose took advantage of his absence to study the garden. The neatly cut grass put her patch to shame. There were no dandelions and no humpy bits. Still, they probably had a gardener. To the side of the house was a walkway, about five feet wide, bordered by hardy shrubs. Projecting from the building was a balcony, the ornate iron rail newly painted. On the paving stones, Rose saw what appeared to be one of the white damask tablecloths. She really ought to wear her glasses more often although her slight short-sightedness was no real handicap.

Strolling towards it in order to retrieve it, Rose munched some celery filled with cream cheese and garlic. Then she froze.

'Oh, God. Oh, my God.' She threw the paper plate and its contents into the shrubbery and ran towards the crumpled figure of Gabrielle Milton.

Rose took three deep breaths to steady herself. There was blood on the ground, oozing slowly from a head wound but already coagulating. She felt for a pulse, knowing in advance she would not find one. Gabrielle was on her side; one glassy eye stared at Rose through the strands of her hair.

Her own pulse racing, she went to find Dennis who came outside at once.

His face white with shock, he rang immediately for an ambulance. It was the instinctive thing to do, even though his wife was dead. 'And the police, I think,' Rose said quietly.

Almost incoherent, Dennis had the job of explaining the situation to his guests. 'There's been an accident,' he said. 'Gabrielle . . . she's, well, she's fallen from the balcony. I think she might be dead.' Impossible to admit it was so.

Rose heard a small scream. A male voice said, 'Shit.' Then for several seconds there was utter silence.

Rose was amazed to hear her own voice, loud and authoritative. 'I think it would be better if we all stayed in here.'

Perhaps because she was alongside Dennis the guests assumed she was closer to the family than she really was. Whatever their reasons, those who had been about to go outside remained in their places. 'An ambulance and the police are on their way,' she continued, realising everyone was waiting for someone to say something, to take charge of a situation which was in danger of taking on nightmare proportions.

Doreen Clarke helped shepherd the people who were still outside into the lounge. She had seen Rose's pallor when she rounded the corner on her way back to the house. She had also seen the way the young woman named Maggie Anderson had been looking at her employer.

Doreen Clarke busied herself clearing away empty dishes and generally tidying up the area where the food had been served. It was unlikely anyone would want to eat now. Rose Trevelyan, she thought, wasn't at all what she had imagined. She had seen a couple of articles about her in *The Cornishman* and recognised her from the photographs. For some reason she had imagined she would be a bit above herself. In the flesh she seemed quite nice. And she'd certainly handled things sensibly.

Doreen had spoken to her husband, Cyril, about the lady painter but he, in his usual way, had just grunted. Cyril didn't fool her, Doreen knew he took in every word she said even if he chose to ignore most of them.

Doreen knew that Mrs Milton had not fallen off that balcony.

She resisted the temptation to creep round the side and folded the tablecloths ready for the laundry, wondering if, or for how long, her services would now be required.

'Please, everyone, have another drink.' Dennis was becoming more agitated with every minute that passed, aware that no one knew quite what to say. And should he, as her husband, be keeping vigil by the body? Of course he should, but he could not bear to see his wife like that.

'Where's Eileen?'

As he spoke she came back into the room. By the puzzled expression on her face she was apparently oblivious to what had happened. 'Pour everyone a drink, Eileen. A large one.' Dennis's hand trembled as his own glass was refilled.

Detective Inspector Pearce had commandeered several rooms and the process of interviewing the guests individually had begun. It was late but no one had been allowed to leave.

Outside a team of forensic experts were at work and through the curtains of the small room at the side of the house the pop of flash-bulbs could be seen.

Rose, being the person to find the body, was the first to be interviewed.

Detective Inspector Pearce seemed to have no consideration for the shock Rose had received. His questions were direct and demanded answers. She had none to give. Barely able to remember what she had done or even if she had screamed, she described the event as best she could.

'Yes, I did touch her. I felt for a pulse. In her wrist,' Rose added hastily. She could not have fumbled beneath the thick dark hair for the carotid artery and endured the stickiness of Gabrielle's blood on her hands. She was, Rose realised, being treated as a suspect.

'You were a close friend of Mrs Milton?' Inspector Pearce studied the woman who sat opposite him. Mrs Trevelyan. And she wore a wedding ring. But there was no Mr Trevelyan on the guest list Doreen Clarke had provided.

'No. I hardly knew her.'

'Oh?'

'I did a job for her. Mrs Milton telephoned me and asked if I'd like to come tonight. I don't go to parties very often. I thought . . . well, I thought it would make a change.' I do not need to explain myself to this man, she told herself.

'This job, what was it exactly?'

'Christmas cards. Mrs Milton wanted a picture of the house to be mounted on personalised cards. I brought the proofs with me tonight.' Rose felt ashamed as she briefly wondered if she would ever be paid for the job. But it had been the same during David's illness: trivial things had worried her, she had been irritated by minor inconveniences and her thoughts, at times, had been irrational. All of it, she guessed, had been a defence mechanism at work to prevent her dwelling on the reality of what was ahead.

DI Pearce, Rose concluded when she finally met his gaze, had the eyes of a dead haddock. She was trembling, her hands clasped tightly together in her lap, and despite the warmth of the evening she was cold. A horrifying idea crossed her mind. Was this a punishment? Had Gabrielle died and Rose been the one to find her body because she was enjoying herself instead of staying at home grieving over the anniversary of David's death? Was she to be the harbinger of tragedy for everyone with whom she came into contact? Only now, almost an hour after the discovery of the body, did the enormity of the situation hit her. Her trembling limbs began to shake, her head and hands suddenly felt clammy and waves of nausea washed over her. 'I'm going to be sick,' she said and promptly vomited on the carpet.

'Get Mrs Trevelyan some water, sergeant.' DI Pearce addressed the man in jeans and a short-sleeved shirt who sat beside him. 'And something to clean up with. Do you feel better now?'

'Yes, thank you. I didn't mean . . . I'm so sorry.' Rose had no reason to apologise. It was not her interrogator's house, nor was it his carpet. Gabrielle Milton lay dead outside on the paving stones; her being sick was a small matter by comparison. And the man hadn't flinched. He had shown no expression of annoyance or disgust but accepted what had happened as if it was a daily occurrence. Rose decided his emotions matched his appearance.

Sipping the water she tried to hide her face behind the glass as Sergeant Walters got to work with a bucket and cloth. She would not humiliate herself further by offering to clean up.

It was strange. She had not wanted David to die but had cursed at death for being so leisurely because of his pain. Although she believed she was prepared for the end, in reality she had not been. This was so different, so unexpected and hard to accept. She would never get to know Gabrielle Milton now.

'What was the party in aid of?'

'Nothing in particular. I think Mrs Milton just wanted to break the ice with people, to feel a part of things. I think, perhaps, she was lonely.'

'You said you didn't know her. Did she tell you that?'

'No. It was just an impression I had.'

'I am not here to seek impressions, Mrs Trevelyan, only facts.'

'Then am I free to go? I've given you all the facts I'm aware of.' There was some satisfaction in the way Inspector Pearce's eyebrows arched fractionally. He was not completely devoid of feelings after all.

Before she left, Rose was made to go through it all

again. To catch her out? she wondered. She said she was fit enough to go home. The taxi they had ordered earlier to collect them had been cancelled. Rose asked if she could use the telephone to rebook it. 'Half an hour,' Pearce told her. He knew she had come with Mr Rowe but he still had to be interviewed.

'What's going on back there?' the driver asked when he arrived. He had been made to wait at the gate by a PC monitoring comings and goings.

'We're not allowed to discuss it,' Barry said firmly, which was true. Even in the poor illumination of street lights he saw how pale Rose was and took her hand and squeezed it, but he made no attempt at conversation. They were silent throughout the drive. Outside her house Barry waited while she found her keys, then asked if she wanted him to come in.

'I could stay if you like?' The offer was made from concern for Rose, there was no ulterior motive.

Rose understood that but she needed to be alone, to rid her mind of images she hoped one day would fade completely.

'No, thanks, Barry. I'll be fine. Really.'

'OK. But don't hesitate to ring if you need to talk, no matter what the time is.' Barry, too, was aware how close it was to the date of David's death. For the evening to have ended as it had was the last thing Rose needed when she was trying to socialise in the way she had when David was alive.

Once inside the kitchen Rose started shaking again.

She had had three fair-sized glasses of wine but was totally sober now. Her hands were like ice as she uncorked the brandy and slopped some into a tumbler. And then, for reasons unknown to herself, she went into the sitting-room and unplugged the telephone.

The brandy warmed her, its effects, on her now empty stomach, felt immediately. She rinsed the glass and went to bed. But sleep evaded her. Rose had told Inspector Pearce she had last seen Gabrielle ten minutes or so before Doreen Clarke had announced that the food was ready. Because she did not know everyone present it had been difficult to say who had or had not been in the lounge or near the buffet table before she had decided to inspect the garden. Eileen, the thin woman serving the drinks, had disappeared, Doreen Clarke had presumably been seeing to the food, the tallish, slim woman with auburn hair who seemed to be on her own had vanished, likewise Paul and his fiancée, Anna. There were approximately forty people present; she could not be expected to know all their whereabouts. Fortunately she had been able to confirm that Barry was at the end of one of the trestle tables chatting with Mike and Barbara Phillips and, as most of the guests knew the doctor, they would not be under any real suspicion. Suspicion? Rose suddenly realised what she had somehow known all along. Gabrielle Milton's death was no accident. So what, she thought as she tossed and turned, had the woman done to attract such dislike that someone wanted her dead?

* * *

Doreen Clarke's duties were supposed to end at ten thirty, by which time the guests would have eaten. Any remaining food was to be neatly rearranged and left in the kitchen to be eaten later, if required. Cyril Clarke had been turned away at the gates and told to come back for his wife later.

When she was finally allowed to leave she had remained silent throughout the drive home, mystifying her husband further. Once at the cottage she had said she felt ill and, after filling a hot water bottle, had gone straight to bed. She was asleep when Cyril joined her half an hour later. Doreen, he realised, coped with things her own way. Major catastrophes not only silenced her tongue but allowed her eight or nine hours' sleep, three more than she was accustomed to. Anxiety or stress caused some people to eat more or less than was usual, not so his wife, but the extra hours of rest did not make her any more tolerant.

Cyril rose at seven to another sunny day although the thermometer in his small greenhouse showed it had been chilly in the night and there was an autumnal feeling in the early morning air. Satisfied that no plague of destructive insects had destroyed his plants, Cyril inspected the last of the tomatoes growing against the side of the cottage. They were still green and hard, and he decided they probably wouldn't ripen now. Doreen might as well have them to make chutney. Cyril Clarke, ex-miner, had taken quite a few years to come to terms with things above the earth's surface. With the closure of Geever mine came the end of life as he, and his ancestors, had known it. For him, and many others, there was no work to be found. Moving away was not a consideration. He and Doreen were Cornish-born, had never lived anywhere else and could not bear the thought of doing so. It was Doreen who had kept things going by doing other women's housework. Now he had his pension things were a little easier. Cyril, for want of something to do, had taken to putting things into the ground rather than digging tin out. There was a sense of achievement in being able to hand Doreen a head of lettuce or some peas or potatoes. It was cheaper than buying vegetables and the excess he sold to local shops. His pocket money, he called it.

He did not hear Doreen get up. She watched her husband from the back door as he peered at the undersides of the leaves on the rose bushes. His grey, grizzled hair was covered with a cap which he wore winter and summer. Doreen reckoned all those years in a miner's helmet made him feel naked when his head was uncovered.

'Cyril!'

'Dear God, woman. You gave me a fright.' The secateurs had clattered to the path.

Doreen, despite the sleep, was pale through her tan, her eyes heavy and her fading blonde hair untidy. 'Cyril, we're not supposed to talk about it, but I can't not tell you. You won't say anything, will you?'

'Of course not, love. What is it?' He approached her and smiled gently.

'She's dead. Mrs Milton. She's been murdered. Oh, they say she might've fallen off the balcony, but I know better. The railing's waist-high. Besides, she doesn't drink, not more than the odd glass, so it wasn't that.'

'Murdered?' Cyril rubbed his newly shaved chin. It seemed impossible, with the sun shining and birds singing, that such a thing could have happened to mar the peace of the village. Despite his wife's foibles he loved her and he did not doubt that what she said was true. She had stuck with him through the bad times, put up with less money and his own frustration and occasional bouts of bad temper which were the result of having no job. Once he had reached the official retirement age when his job would have ended anyway, he had come to terms with life. He had also come to terms with Doreen. He saw now that this was no hyperbolic description of some incident she had witnessed.

'Come on, let's go in and we'll talk about it.' He took her arm and lowered her into a kitchen chair, then plugged in the kettle. It was cool inside, the sun not having moved far enough from the east to be visible from the windows.

'I couldn't keep it from you, Cyril. We've never had any secrets in the past. It's just the thought that someone there did it, that's what gets me. To think I may have served them food.' Doreen shook her head. 'What'll we do if Mr Milton doesn't want to keep the place and the new people decide they don't want me?'

'Oh, Dor, it doesn't matter. Really it doesn't.' He put an arm around her shoulder and kissed the top of her head. 'We'll cope.' But he had a rough idea of what she was going through, he had been through it himself. And on top of that was the thought that someone they knew might be capable of murder.

CHAPTER FOUR

Inspector Pearce knew it would be foolish to assume someone who had attended the party was Gabrielle Milton's killer, although it seemed most likely. There was the possibility that the party, with guests and cars arriving randomly, had been used to disguise the arrival of someone else whose presence would have been noticed at any other time by curious, nosy or suspicious neighbours. Cornish himself, Jack Pearce was aware that strangers were summed up and not accepted until they had proved themselves to be not wanting.

The hardest part of the job was having to treat people he knew as suspects. Of those present at the Miltons' on Saturday night he knew only Dr Phillips and his wife personally. Barry Rowe he had met two years previously when his printing premises had been broken into. A case, he recalled, which had never been solved.

It would be up to his counterparts in the Met to make inquiries into Mrs Milton's London connections. She had not lived in Cornwall for long enough to rule them out. Meanwhile he had to concentrate on the guests and those with whom she had come into contact locally. And in seven months they numbered quite a lot. There had been builders and decorators, electricians and plumbers, delivery men and tradesmen, each of whom had helped turn the house from a draughty, expensive place to run into the luxurious residence it now was.

The expression 'house-to-house inquiries' seemed ludicrous in that the Miltons had very few neighbours, but someone had killed her and someone, somewhere, may have noticed something unusual. He sent the men at his disposal to find out.

Eileen Penrose was still recovering from her ordeal when someone from CID came to interview her husband. She had been uncooperative during her initial interview, claiming she had been too busy serving drinks and looking after the guests to notice anything that had happened during the evening. Asked where she had been when Mr Milton had decided everyone had better have another drink she had replied, 'Where do you think I was? Everyone needs to use the bathroom at some point.' But not upstairs, she had insisted, the facilities there were en suite with the bedrooms. There was a downstairs cloakroom for guests and staff. She had not lied but there were things she had omitted from her statement.

As far as Eileen Penrose was concerned, she would shed no tears over the death of someone she considered to be a rival.

'He's out,' she said sharply when the detective constable knocked on the door. 'And I've only just got in myself.'

It was now possible for the police to be more open in their questioning, having ascertained that Gabrielle Milton's only relations were all present at the party and no one else needed informing of her death.

Eileen narrowed her eyes and crossed her arms over her scrawny chest, partly to disguise the thudding of her heart which she was sure could be heard. Her sigh of relief was barely audible when she learnt it was Jim the man wanted to see. 'He wasn't even there,' she told him.

'We know that, Mrs Penrose, but we have to speak to everyone who's been to the Milton place.'

'My Jim saw to their heating system, if that's what you mean. I can tell you where he is if you need to speak to him right away.'

The young constable already pitied Jim Penrose and bet his pinched-looking wife demanded to know where he was every minute of the day. 'I've got other people to see. What time are you expecting him back?'

'Twelve thirty. For his dinner.'

'Thank you.' Before he had taken the two steps down from the front door it was closed.

Eileen went straight to the cupboard over the sink and took down a bottle of sweet sherry which was only ever used in trifles and gravy and poured an inch or so into a glass. Had anyone else done this, taken a drink in their own home in the middle of the morning, she would have claimed they were two steps away from being alcoholic.

She prayed no one had seen her on that day and wished now she had kept her mouth shut instead of letting Maureen know she thought Jim was up to something with Mrs Milton. Feeling calmer, she hung out the washing, looking forward to watching Jim's face when it was his turn to be questioned. 'That'll give him something to chew on,' she muttered. 'Teach him to mess about with other women. Serves him right if he's arrested.' But what she had seen worried her.

Rose woke from a fitful sleep with a headache. Catching sight of her face in the dressing-table mirror on her way to the bathroom, she found it ironic that she had expected to look and feel this way after the party, but for different reasons. The headache, she guessed, was caused by lack of sleep and an empty stomach. Yesterday she had eaten little, not wanting to spoil her appetite for later, and what she had eaten had not stayed inside her for long.

Once she had showered and cleaned her teeth she felt marginally better. Downstairs she pulled back the curtains. A sea fret hung over the bay like a veil. Only the tip of St Michael's Mount was visible; Lizard Point was totally obscured. The unbelievable shades of blue of the sea were not in evidence. Today it was a milky green. Two trawlers were making their way of out of the harbour and in the middle distance a salvage tug, rolling fractionally on a swell, hovered like a vulture, its owners and crew hoping for the worst.

Rose never knew what to expect when she drew the sitting-room curtains. The light and shade were ever-changing, the bay might or might not be busy. Now and then numerous sails would fill the far end of the bay where the yacht club was situated. Here was where she had finally understood the meaning of the word chiaroscuro. Light and shade. Here was so different from the memories of her childhood holidays, spent with her parents out of season in resorts such as Brighton and Great Yarmouth where the sea was the colour of dental amalgam and layers of clothes were required to keep out the biting wind and bursts of rain.

Rose lit the grill of the gas cooker – the toaster had packed up several months ago – and allowed it to heat up. She felt she needed pampering so made coffee in the filter machine rather than instant. She opened the kitchen door, which was at the side of the house and led to the small garden. To the right was a rocky cliff face, ahead was the lawn bordered by hardy shrubs and tubs of plants. To the left was the open vista of the bay, seen from the sitting-room and her bedroom, but not from the kitchen. A herring-gull appeared to be performing some secret ritual as it side-stepped first one way then the other along the narrow ridge of the sloping roof of the shed, ignoring the mewing cries of the immature birds beside it. The gull and its mate had nested for the second year in the angle of the chimney stack on her roof.

Rose ate two slices of toast and butter and was drinking her second cup of coffee when the news came on. There were brief details concerning Gabrielle Milton's death which, the announcer said, the police were treating as suspicious. She had been right, then. Rose did not believe Gabrielle had simply fallen.

Poor Dennis, she thought. But it was the reactions of both Paul and Anna which she had found interesting. They were shocked, certainly, but not distraught and they had exchanged a look she could not guess the meaning of. And the auburn-haired woman – there had been a gleam of something Rose could only think of as satisfaction when Dennis had broken the news. No, she told herself, pouring a third cup of coffee. It is not my concern. The fish-eyed inspector would sort it out. He would, he had told her, probably need to speak to her again and had written down her address. Well, it won't be this morning, Rose decided, because I'm going out. She set off in the car.

The tide was perfect, on the turn, leaving bare the shiny mud of the Hayle estuary where many birds were feeding. Barry Rowe liked her bird paintings. They were not accurate, detailed representations but shaded impressions of shape and line. She laid down a waterproof sheet and sat down to work.

A slight breeze lifted her hair and soughed through the grasses behind her. There were few people in sight from the spot she had chosen and after this weekend there would be fewer still. The holiday season was coming to an end. In the distance cars crawled along the narrow road but the only sounds were rustlings and the occasional whistling call of an oyster-catcher.

An hour and a half later, feeling stiff, Rose packed away her things and decided to walk along the bank. The tide was coming in now. She continued on to where the shops started and crossed the bridge over the estuary and followed the road up into the Towans. Here, steep banks of the well-advertised golden sand had been warmed by the sun and trickled down the backs of her calves as she descended a path trodden by other feet between the waving marram grass on to the flat sweep of the sands. The sky was clear, the sea a darker blue, almost turquoise; there was no sign of the damp mist which hung over Mount's Bay and which could do so for days on end whilst everywhere else remained sunny. A frill of white foam separated sea from sand. Rose walked until her legs ached and she realised she still had to get back to the car.

Yesterday's guilt had disappeared. Rose was thinking more of the murder than of David, and of the strangers she had met. She was hungry again so she decided to go straight home, stopping only once at the Co-op in Newlyn for milk and some tomatoes. She had to wait to be served. A crew from a fishing boat had two trolleys to be checked out but she was not in a hurry.

'Zat all you got, maid?' One of the older men nodded towards her two items. 'You gwon then.'

'Cheers.' Rose smiled and handed over the right money.

The shock of finding Gabrielle was wearing off but Rose knew it would take at least another twenty-four hours. Work had helped to take her mind off it and she knew Barry would be pleased with her efforts. The bird scenes he used on cards left blank for the sender to write their own message.

Taking a doorstep sandwich containing cheese and salad up to the attic, Rose decided she would continue to work. Hopefully she would be able to fall into bed exhausted tonight and sleep properly. It was an advantage of being her own boss that it did not matter if she slept late in the mornings.

Another idea of Barry's had been to photograph churches, buildings which abounded in Cornwall and ranged from picturesque to Gothic to the no-nonsense style of the Methodists. The singing of hymns by the whole congregation had appealed to the Cornish; consequently John Wesley, who had introduced this idea, had left his mark by adding to the Methodist influence. Rose had agreed to Barry's suggestion and had added that they would be more striking in black and white matt. There was a roll of undeveloped film awaiting attention. Barry required them for a trade fair and thought they would make alternative Easter cards. Although he was in business to make money, like Rose he hated the commercial aspects of the two main religious festivals. 'Go on,' he had urged. 'I know how much you despise yellow chicks and bunnies. The most you can lose is a film.'

Leaning forward to catch a slice of tomato in danger of sliding out of her sandwich, Rose remembered she had left the proofs of the Milton photographs at the house. She might not have been allowed to retrieve them, she thought cynically; DI Pearce might consider them as evidence.

The work completed, Rose slid the first of the church shots under the enlarger, then decided against it. The pictures would lose their stark impact if they were made bigger. Let Barry decide, she thought. Before she went downstairs again she took out her own copies of the photographs she had taken for Gabrielle. Something troubled her but she could not remember what it was. She kept copies of everything in clearly marked folders in a filing cabinet, both for her own reference and in case a client desired a further order.

The sun was an orange globe by the time she was seated in the armchair nearest the window, a small table beside it. She had neglected Laura, whom she had promised to ring to tell her how the party went – although she was surprised Laura had not contacted her. Surely she must have heard the news? But Laura was out.

Six thirty. It was not too early for a glass of wine. She poured one and returned to the sitting-room. The first shots of the Milton house were what she expected. It was the last one which puzzled her. It took several minutes before she realised what it was.

On the far right-hand side was a minute blur.

Rose picked up a magnifying glass but whatever it was became no clearer. When she had released the shutter the final time she had registered a movement. When she stepped back from the camera Dilys had gone. 'But Dilys', she said aloud, 'must have fled immediately after the picture was taken.' Because in that picture Dilys was still there. Standing, it was true, ready to jump, but there all the same. Rose doubted the enlarger would clarify the blur if the magnifying glass had not done so.

'Barry,' she said, having dialled his number, ashamed that she expected him both to be in and to respond to her wishes. 'How about that drink I owe you?'

'I was just about to ring you. I thought I'd leave it until this evening to give you a chance to . . . well, to rest.' He wasn't sure what he meant, only that he had guessed Rose would prefer to be on her own.

'Rest? Oh, yes, I see.' Was it selfish to have been working all day under the circumstances? 'I need someone to talk to. Are you busy?' she added hastily.

'No. And I'm your man.' I'm never too busy where you're concerned, he thought, but he could never say the words aloud. He did not want to lose whatever he had with Rose, as little as it was.

'Look, why don't I meet you somewhere? Are you at the shop?' Barry's calls were automatically transferred from the shop to his flat. Throughout the summer he opened on Sundays.

'No. I closed at six. I can pick you up.'

'I need the walk.' Her earlier ennui had worn off.

They arranged to meet outside his flat.

Rose was pale with dark semicircles under her eyes. 'Where would you like to go?'

'I don't mind.'

Barry's flat was situated in a side street which led off the Promenade. They strolled down to the bottom and turned left, crossing the road at the pedestrian lights directly in front of the long glass frontage of the Queen's Hotel. Rose realised she wasn't as strong as she had believed. 'The Navy?' she suggested. It was a small, friendly pub just off the sea front.

To the left of the door was a pool table, tucked away in its own space. The bar itself formed three sides of a rectangle and there were individual tables around the walls. They carried their drinks to a secluded area at the back. Barry did not comment that Rose had offered to pay. It seemed she had forgotten.

'There's something not quite right,' she said. 'Look, what I told you about that woman, the one that Dennis kept looking at . . .'

'Maggie.'

'Maggie?'

'Maggie Anderson. She introduced herself to me when you went walkabout.'

'Did she?' Rose turned in her chair and stared at Barry with new respect. Maggie was an extremely attractive female. Barry could not be described as handsome but he had a nice face; a kind face, if a little lived-in. His hair was thinning on top and his heavy-framed glasses kept slipping down. It was a characteristic gesture of his to be constantly pushing them back in place. 'Well, do you think I should have said anything to the police? About my suspicions, I mean?'

'Good heavens, Rose.' Barry laughed. 'Certainly not. You've met Gabrielle Milton only once, you don't know her husband and you certainly can't go around accusing people you've never set eyes on of having an affair.'

Rose felt herself blushing. That was the trouble with Barry. Although she suspected he was half in love with her he had no qualms about putting her straight. 'All right, what about this then.' From her handbag she produced the photograph of the house with Dilys ready to spring.

'What about it?' Barry nudged his glasses and frowned.

'There. Can't you see?'

'It's blurred, if that's what you mean.'

'Quite. And I'm sure I saw something move. And it wasn't the cat like I thought at first.'

'Rose, what are you trying to do? You can't get involved, you know, and you're seeing things that aren't there. I know this isn't an easy time for you but you know nothing about the Miltons and their friends, and a tiny blur in a picture doesn't mean anything. Probably it was the wind disturbing something.'

'There was no wind.' Rose stared straight ahead,

annoyed with Barry and with herself for being stupid.

'Leave it to the police.' But Barry took a second look. Between the shrubs was what he thought might be, if he allowed his imagination a free hand, the blurred image of a female body in profile. 'It could be', he said, thinking aloud without meaning to encourage Rose, 'Gabrielle. You know, getting out of the way if she realised she might end up on the front of her Christmas cards.'

'She was in the house.' Rose replaced the picture in her bag. But she was smiling. Barry had seen it too.

'I did notice something last night.'

'Which was?'

'The son, Paul, he kept trying to attract his father's attention. Like he was agitated about something.'

'He probably was. He and Anna were rowing. Drink up, it's my round.'

Barry watched Rose as she approached the bar. Her figure was neat in a straight denim skirt and slimmer by half a stone, lost when David died and never regained. Her bare legs were brown and, from behind, with her faded auburn hair in an untidy pony tail, she looked like a much younger woman. He had been too slow in asking her out, he recalled. It was David who had stepped in and now it was too late. Rose treated him like a friend; he would never be more than that.

Barry was aware what people thought of him even if they kept these thoughts to themselves. 'Boring,' he muttered. 'And it's true.' It was as if the burning passions which drove men to great heights or the depths of despair had passed him by, but he was still able to feel a twinge of jealousy when other men looked at Rose.

'Thanks,' he said when Rose returned with their drinks. 'Have you eaten?'

'I'm not hungry.' The sandwich lay heavily in her stomach, the nausea of the previous evening not far away. Work, and trying to make something out of a stupid photograph, had, she realised, been a way of trying to forget what she had seen. Delayed shock was setting in.

'Well, I am.' He studied the menu in its red leather cover. There was a large selection but Rose knew he would, as always, order one of Marg's, the landlady's, home-made pasties. She could only eat half of one herself.

'Rose,' Barry said later, when he had walked her home. 'Just try and forget what happened. It wasn't as if we knew them.'

But that, to Rose, was the whole point. It had been another missed opportunity in her life.

CHAPTER FIVE

Dennis Milton had spent most of Sunday at Camborne police station where the questioning, along with shock and grief, had taken its toll. He knew that as her husband he was considered to be the main suspect, but surely enough people had been able to say he was either in the lounge or on the patio the whole evening?

He was allowed to return to the house but his bedroom was still out of bounds. Forensic experts had gone over it and would probably do so again. For the time being the door was taped.

It had been confirmed that Gabrielle had fallen from the balcony but the police refused to tell him why they were certain she had been pushed.

Anna had also been questioned at length but told she was free to return to London as long as she remained at the address she had given. She returned by train as Paul had volunteered to stay with Dennis.

On Monday morning Doreen Clarke telephoned and asked if her services were needed. Unable to think rationally, Dennis said yes, then spent the rest of the day sitting on the bench at the end of the garden, his eyes averted from the path leading down the side of the house. He was numb, but what was worse was that Gabrielle's death was no accident. And it was unbelievable that she had been there long enough to make an enemy of someone. He refused to face the alternative.

'I don't know what to do about Mrs Trevelyan,' he said to Paul as they picked at the meal Doreen had left for them. 'Do about her?'

'I feel I ought to speak to her. I mean, she found . . . she was the first . . .' He did not want to say it. 'She must be very upset herself.'

Paul shrugged. He had never been an emotional child outwardly but Dennis knew he suffered in his own way. His dark hair made a stark contrast to the paleness of his face and there was a slight tremor in his hands unless they were employed. As an only child the loss of his mother must have come hard. Dennis suddenly realised he had no idea how to comfort Paul.

'I'm sorry, I can't finish this,' he told Doreen when she came to clear the plates. She had taken it upon herself to stay for a couple of extra hours but she, too, realised there was little she could do for the Milton men except keep the place tidy and produce food at regular intervals.

'Shall I come tomorrow?' she asked.

Dennis nodded. 'Please.' He could not bear the thought of having only Paul for company.

Rose Trevelyan's number was listed in the telephone book. Dennis lifted the receiver, then changed his mind. The telephone was not a method of communication he favoured; it would be better to speak to Mrs Trevelyan face to face. And it would get him out of the house.

Rose was cleaning her brushes when she heard a knock on the door. She was puzzled – all her friends came round to the side. The police, she decided, as she wiped her hands on the old towel she had tied around her waist. For most of the day she had succeeded in blocking out what she had seen.

'Mr Milton!' She stepped back, surprised. 'I'm sorry. Come in, please.' She showed him into the sitting-room and apologised for her appearance. 'Excuse me just one moment.' There was a jacket potato in the oven, which she turned down, and a piece of steak marinating. She had intended clearing her working areas, then making some salad. On the table near where she had asked Dennis to sit down was a bottle of red wine, open, and a glass beside it. It was too late to hide it and she wondered why she felt she should have. Ought she to have written a note of condolence? People had been so good to her when David died, but what did you say to a man whose wife had been murdered?

'Would you like a drink? I've just opened a bottle.' Rose bit her lip. This, then, was what you said.

'I . . . er, yes. If you're having one.'

Rose fetched another glass and filled both, stopping herself in time from saying 'Cheers'. They sat opposite each other, either side of the fireplace. Dennis was in David's chair but that did not hurt her any longer. Rose took the initiative and broke the awkward silence. 'I should have telephoned,' she said. 'I'm sorry. But I didn't know what to say. I know I hardly knew her, but I liked Gabrielle. How's your son taking it?'

Dennis ran a hand through his thinning sandy hair which he wore swept back from his forehead. His stubby fingers, Rose noticed, were freckled. 'I don't know. He hasn't said a lot. It's a terrible thing to admit, Mrs Trevelyan, but somewhere over the years we've drifted apart.'

'Rose.'

'Rose, then. I suppose it started when we sent him away to school. Gabrielle was against it. I . . .' He stopped again. He seemed unable to take a thought through to its full conclusion. Every now and then the reality that he would never see his wife again hit him. It was like being winded. 'I struggle to make conversation with him. What do you think I should do?' He made eye contact for the first time.

Rose found it odd that this recently bereaved virtual stranger should be sitting in her house asking her advice. She gazed out over the bay. A purplish dusk was falling and the lights of Newlyn harbour flickered on. There was no inspiration there.

'Perhaps if you sat down and really talked to him, told him what you've just told me. He probably feels the same.'

'Yes.'

But Rose was not sure if he had even heard her.

'I felt I had to come. To make sure you were all right.' Dennis meant it but underneath he saw that, because Rose had found Gabrielle's body, a sort of bond existed between them.

'Please don't worry about me, Dennis, you've got enough to think about. Have the police gone yet?'

'No. They're still in and out and they've got one of their van things parked at the front. They said it was fortunate that most of the guests were local. Fortunate.' He spat the word. 'For them, maybe. Not for Gabrielle.'

Rose studied his face as he sipped his drink. There were lines of fatigue and strain but it was a pleasant, almost handsome face. Something told her there was more than his wife's death on his mind.

'I'm in a bit of a mess,' he said, as if he had telepathic powers.

'Oh?'

'Who wouldn't be?' he said quickly, unaware he had spoken aloud. 'You have a nice place here. This is the sort of thing I imagined Gabrielle wanted, something with more of a family feeling than our London flat.'

Rose saw the room properly for the first time in ages. It was far too long since she had decorated and the floral covers of the suite were fading. She could never have drawn the curtains, shutting out the sun and the view, to prevent it happening. Now, she thought, was not the time to be thinking of soft furnishings.

'I love it here. So did my husband. He died four years ago tomorrow. Of cancer.'

Dennis's expression was sympathetic. He guessed she wanted to reassure him that he was not the only one to suffer, that life would go on regardless.

'Would you like some more wine?' Rose was thankful she preferred the skin of baked potatoes crispy. Dennis seemed oblivious to the warm cooking smell which was drifting in from the kitchen.

'Please. And the view. It's amazing. The whole bay. That was another thing I couldn't understand, moving down here and looking out at sand dunes and gorse. You can just see the sea in the distance. And the extra bedrooms when Gabrielle made it clear she didn't want people coming down from London all the time. God, listen to me. I didn't mean to criticise.'

'Perhaps it was the space she wanted.' Rose meant mentally as well as physically. She could understand it. When she had to spend a couple of days in London the first thing she did upon her return was to walk. She'd take a cliff path and surround herself with sea and sky and breathe in the clean air.

Dennis bowed his head. 'I loved her, you know. Despite everything, I really loved that woman. And now I shall have to sell the house that she loved.'

Rose braced herself. Had Dennis been drinking?

Surely two glasses of mediocre wine was not enough to make him maudlin. She recognised the difference between that and genuine grief. Grief, she knew, had no time for sentimentality. Grief was hard and sharp, the pain almost physical. It was tempered with cleansing anger.

Dennis, she suspected, was working himself up to making a confession and she would put money on her assumption that he was having an affair.

'I didn't know many of the guests, they were mostly people Gabrielle had met, but I feel responsible somehow, for putting them through this, all these questions. God, what a mess.' Dennis shook his head. 'Look, I've taken up enough of your time already. I really must go.' He placed his empty glass on the table and stood. 'Thank you, Rose, for listening. I won't bother you again.'

She saw him to the door and watched as he pulled away, his headlights sweeping through the darkness until the car had disappeared.

Rose put the steak under the grill and wondered if it had been an act, if Dennis Milton had killed his wife and was trying to put himself in a good light with people. Her natural curiosity made her want to find out more about the Miltons. Something, definitely, was not quite right.

Maggie Anderson had provided the police with her home address and that of her place of work. Like Anna, after endless questions, she had been allowed to return to

71

London. She had explained that she had known Dennis for about eighteen months, which was true, that they had met through business and that her being at the party was probably to redress the balance. Almost everyone else was a friend of Gabrielle's.

'It's over,' Maggie told herself when she boarded the train on Sunday evening. She had not had to lie but she had omitted many points. If they checked, the police would discover that Dennis's company was once a client of the advertising agency for whom she worked. And they would check, she was sure.

The train swayed through the darkness, stopping at all the stations until it reached Plymouth. Leaving Cornwall behind, she sighed with relief.

Saturday night had been spent under Dennis's roof, as had been the case with several of the guests. By the time the police had finished with them it was too late to go to bed and no one felt like sleeping. Maggie, along with two couples she did not know, remained in the lounge, resting as best they could on the settees. She had reserved a room in a hotel although she had hoped she would be invited to spend the night – not that Dennis would have issued the invitation. The matter was taken out of her hands.

It was hard to feel sorry for Gabrielle. The obstacle to Maggie's plans had now been removed.

Analysing her feelings, Maggie knew she was not in love with Dennis but he represented everything she wanted from life. He had money and power and knew how to use them although he had been unaware of her manipulation of the situation. Inexpensive restaurants had been chosen with care, the better to show herself in contrast to what she imagined was Gabrielle's extravagance. Gabrielle's contentment with books and her renewed enthusiasm for broadening her mind were not known to Maggie. But Dennis refused to discuss his wife with her.

Now, of course, it was only a matter of time before she got what she wanted.

'What do you think?'

'I think you're crazy.' Laura was studying the enlargements Rose had made of the view of the Milton house, concentrating on the right-hand side of the photographs. 'It's just a blur. It could be anything.' But Laura was prepared to humour Rose today. She had not forgotten the date. 'Does it matter?'

'I don't know. Barry agrees with me, though.'

'Ah.' Laura grinned. 'Barry would.'

'Should I show it to the police?'

'What for? It was days before she was killed. Besides, it's probably the gardener or Doreen.'

The idea of a gardener had not crossed Rose's mind. 'You know Doreen?'

'Of course I do. She was at school with . . .' Laura ran a hand through her dark curls. 'I keep forgetting you weren't at school with us. Shows how you've become part of the scenery.'

'Doreen's the same age as you?'

'Yes. Hard to believe, isn't it?' She was not being vain – it was simply that Doreen looked years older than her age. 'Could be to do with marrying a man some years her senior, but she doesn't seem to bother what she looks like.'

Nor do I these days, Rose thought, looking down at the worn jeans. 'What's she like? The first time I met her she gave me the creeps.'

'What? Doreen? She's all right. She resents outsiders, that's all, and to her you'll always be one.'

'But she worked for the Miltons and they've only just moved here.'

'That's different. There's money involved. She's had to keep Cyril for years now since the mine closed down. Rose? You're not thinking she killed her, are you?'

Rose shrugged. 'Well, I didn't, nor did Barry. Why not her?'

'When I said crazy, I meant it. You're not thinking of acting detective, are you? Anyway, I don't see any signs of liquid refreshment. What's up with you, woman?'

Rose looked at her depleted wine rack. There was enough for tonight.

Laura was studying the few lines in a national newspaper which were all Gabrielle's death seemed to warrant. Once it would have made headlines. There were times when Rose envied Laura, with three grown-up children and two grandchildren; at others she was glad she had not had any. She was better able to enjoy the years she had with David alone.

'What is it?' Laura glanced up and caught Rose smiling.

'I was thinking of you as a grandmother. It doesn't seem possible.'

'Come on, we're supposed to be deciding where we're going at the weekend.' Trevor would be at sea, Laura and Rose would have a night out.

'There's a film – God, who's that?' Rose frowned. The front door again. Had Dennis Milton decided to pay another visit?

Standing on the bottom of the three steps, and thus appearing the same height as Rose, was Inspector Pearce. 'I wondered when you'd turn up,' she said, realising she sounded rude but not caring. 'Come in.'

'Well, well,' Laura said from her chair at the kitchen table. 'They've put you in charge, have they?'

Rose looked from one to the other. Was there anyone Laura didn't know?

'Another of your school chums?'

'No. But his sister was. How are you, Jack?'

'Fine. You?'

'Surviving. I was just leaving.'

'But . . .' Rose did not have time to complete what she was about to say because Laura had swung her handbag off the back of the chair and waved from the other side of the kitchen door.

Rose took a seat but did not invite her guest to do the same.

'These photographs,' Jack Pearce said without

preamble, 'the ones you claim you delivered to Mrs Milton—'

'I did deliver them,' she interrupted. 'I left them in the small room opposite the lounge.'

'We can't find them.'

'What?'

'They're not in the house.'

'They must be.'

'Are you sure you didn't take them with you? You might've forgotten, you were a bit upset at the time.'

Was he being facetious? 'I did not.'

'Perhaps you left them in the taxi.'

'Look, I know the driver who collected us. I know them all at Stone's Taxis. If I'd done so they would have let me know. And I'm not in the habit of lying, especially to the police.' Rose bit her lip. The man had riled her to the point where she was talking nonsense. The second half of her sentence negated the first.

'Is that so?' DI Pearce's smile was mocking.

'Someone else must've moved them. Mr Milton probably. He wouldn't want a reminder of a Christmas he's not going to be spending with his wife.'

'We've checked.'

'Well, perhaps your men didn't search hard enough.'

The remark was ignored. 'Now you've had a chance to think about it, is there anyone you know who would wish to harm Mrs Milton?'

'I told you at the time, I didn't know her. I spoke to her on the telephone on two occasions and met her once on a business footing. At the party there wasn't much chance to speak to her, she was busy making sure everyone was all right.' But not herself, Rose added silently. 'Is that it? I have got things to do, you know.'

'Hint taken, Mrs Trevelyan. I can see you're very busy.' He dropped his eyes so they rested momentarily on the newspaper spread out on the table and the almost empty bottle of wine.

Rose felt herself blush and opened the kitchen door in a dismissive gesture.

Still annoyed and wondering why she should be, she was not fully aware of what she was saying when the telephone rang. She replaced the receiver, amazed to find she had accepted an invitation for dinner with Dennis Milton.

A stiff breeze rattled the fronds of the palm tree which grew close to the shed. Rose liked the sound they made. It was one of those brilliant September days but colder outside than it appeared. The bank holiday had passed unnoticed for Rose who had missed the Fish Festival, preferring not to have to answer the many questions she would be inundated with by all the people she would see there who knew her.

Whitecaps formed on the tops of the shallow waves as the sea rolled in to Wherrytown Beach. When the tide was higher spray would soak the Promenade and the people foolish enough to think they could time the waves. Sennen, she thought. It would be perfect today.

She could paint the sea as it broke over the rocks. She filled a flask with coffee and was just about to leave when the telephone rang again. 'What now?' she said as she went to answer it.

'Mrs Trevelyan?'

'Yes?' She did not recognise the voice.

'It's Mrs Clarke. Doreen Clarke. From the Milton place. I was wondering if I could have a word with you.'

'Well, I . . . Yes, of course. What is it?'

'Not over the phone. Could I see you? If you're not busy, that is,' she added hastily.

Rose was not exactly busy but she was beginning to feel her life wasn't her own. She was used to solitude and enjoyed it, and she could not imagine that Doreen Clarke had anything to say to her; it was more likely prurient curiosity as to what Rose had discovered on Saturday night. Rather than let her become a nuisance she decided to get it out of the way. 'Where are you?'

'I'm at the Miltons' but I'm leaving in half an hour.'

It was early for her to be finishing whatever she did up there. 'Do you have a car?'

'No. Cyril drops me off. I can get myself over to Penzance easy enough.'

'It's all right. Can you get into Hayle?'

'I don't want to put you to any bother.'

'It's no trouble.' Rose named a tea-shop and cursed herself. She had never been good at saying no but at least she had prevented Doreen from coming to the house.

She loaded what she thought she might need into the car, remembering the flask, then set off.

Doreen Clarke was there before her. But she didn't have as far to come, Rose thought irritably as she entered the cafe. After the cool wind it was warm inside and smelt of coffee and bread and pasties. On the table was a pot of tea. Rose ordered a coffee.

Doreen concentrated on the contents of her teacup until the waitress returned.

'How can I help you, Mrs Clarke?'

Rose waited, watching various expressions cross the woman's face. Her body language suggested she was ill at ease, embarrassed even, but whether that was because she was taking up Rose's time or because of what she had to say, Rose had yet to find out. Doreen fiddled with a teaspoon then dropped it. It clattered against her saucer. Colour spread from her crepey neck into her face.

'Mrs Clarke?'

'I don't think I should be here. I shouldn't have asked you to come.'

Wonderful, Rose thought. A whole morning wasted. 'Well, I am here.' She managed to keep the exasperation out of her voice. Did she need a job, was that it?

'If I tell you, you won't say it came from me, will you?'

'Tell me what?' Until she knew, Rose couldn't answer.

'It's probably no more than stupid gossip.' She took a deep breath and pulled her short, plump body upright in the chair, tucking her straight, grey hair behind her ears.

'Eileen Penrose is a very jealous woman. I've known her for years and it's not just me that realises it. How her husband puts up with her is beyond me.' She lowered her voice as the cafe began to fill up. Two women with children in pushchairs sat behind them, the children making too much noise for them to be overheard. 'She follows him.'

'What?' Rose could not imagine someone doing that.

'She does. Jim did some work for Mrs Milton.'

'Jim?'

'Eileen's husband. He was up there twice. Eileen helps out now and again, but I saw her, you see, about ten days ago it was. I thought you might've seen her too.'

'Me?'

'Yes. You was there, taking the snaps.'

Rose did not explain that what she did was a little more complicated than taking snaps. 'No,' she said firmly. 'I didn't see her.' But maybe she had captured her on film. And in which case, what was she doing there?

'She didn't see me,' Doreen continued. 'But you see, she'd overheard me telling someone in the village that Mrs Milton was having a visitor that afternoon. I think she thought it might be her Jim and she wanted to catch him out. The visitor was you, of course.'

Rose tried to visualise the sort of woman Eileen Penrose must be. Suddenly she realised who Doreen meant. 'Is that the lady who was serving the drinks?'

'Yes.'

Now she understood. Eileen Penrose had been missing

around the time Gabrielle had met her death. 'Did you tell this to the police?'

'No.'

'Why ever not?'

'You don't understand what it's like. She'd never forgive me. Nor would anyone else.'

But Rose did understand. She had lived there long enough to know what a tight-knit community it was, how everyone knew everyone else's business. Doreen Clarke's position would not have been enviable had she mentioned her suspicions. But Rose also saw the advantages. If you weren't seen for a day or so someone would make sure you were all right. 'Why are you telling me?'

'Because you live far enough away. And you were there. And I thought, you being a local celebrity and all, they'd take more notice of you.'

Rose smothered a smile. A local celebrity. So Doreen Clarke already knew or had made inquiries as to who she was. But she did not see how she could bring herself to say all this to Inspector Pearce, although it now seemed likely that it was Eileen Penrose she had captured in that final photograph.

'I can leave it to you then?' Suddenly businesslike, Doreen stood up and fastened her short jacket. She picked up her own bill and took it to the cash desk, leaving Rose trying to decide what she ought to do. Gabrielle Milton's murder, now she was over the initial shock, was beginning to intrigue her.

* * *

81

Dennis Milton was not sure of his motives for asking Rose Trevelyan to dinner but at least it was a way of getting through another night. Paul remained uncommunicative. Dennis had taken Rose's advice and tried to get him to talk, admitting his own faults. Paul had ignored his efforts.

The house seemed larger than ever yet there was no peace. Two men were upstairs now, going through things belonging to Gabrielle that they had not taken away with them. The invasion of her privacy was sickening. Even her handbag was not sacrosanct. Were there, he wondered, secrets she had hidden from him? It was ridiculous feeling the way he did when he had been seeing Maggie, but he was unable to bear the thought that Gabrielle might have met someone else. It could, of course, explain who had killed her. The front door had been left open on the night of the party. It would have been easy for someone to enter the house and wait. If whoever it was was seen – no, Dennis realised that if it was someone local other guests would have known him. Unless it was someone Gabrielle had met in London, in which case everyone would assume it was one of his friends.

He held his head between his hands in despair. It was not his job to find the murderer.

Rose finally made it to Sennen but she was not in the mood to work. Instead she watched the sea. Long, rolling waves gathered momentum and crashed in plumes of white spray over jagged rocks, beyond which water and sky were an identical blue where they met on the horizon. The sight calmed her, made her forget Gabrielle's broken body. The sounds calmed her further: the hiss as the sea sucked at sand the texture of castor sugar, the thud as it hit the rocks. Overhead, gulls screamed like raucous schoolgirls and a black-backed, larger and noisier than the others, made its presence known from the top of the cliff. The wind, coming off the sea, flung her hair wildly round her head and minute grains of sand into her face. Rose breathed deeply, enjoying the salty tang, and felt cleansed. For a few short minutes there was only the present. Then she remembered she was having dinner with Dennis Milton.

She walked back to where she had parked the car, arms folded across her chest, aware that she was chilled. In the driver's seat she poured coffee from the flask, a perfect circle of mist forming on the windscreen from steam from the cup resting on the dashboard. Why, she thought, did Dennis seek her company? Did he suspect she had seen more than she really had, or was he simply lonely?

Rose finished the coffee, tucked her hair, sticky with spray, behind her ears and drove home.

Doreen Clarke had, without consulting Dennis, rearranged her working day. Instead of starting at nine and finishing at one, she was up at the house at eight to cook breakfast and clean, then she went home until it was time to prepare an evening meal. The hours were roughly the same so she did not bother Dennis with discussions about financial alterations. Her motives were not entirely altruistic. She felt sorry for the Miltons and was upset herself but she was looking to her own future. If she made herself indispensable Dennis would want to keep her on. She could take care of the place whilst he was in London, an easy enough task, leaving her time to find other employment as well. She had been surprised when he told her he was expecting Mrs Trevelyan for dinner but had not expressed it. Rose, she was sure, would not mention their earlier conversation.

'Anything in particular you'd like to eat?' Doreen inquired.

'No.' Dennis did not seem to care and most of what she cooked he left.

'You won't say anything, will you?' Doreen whispered to Rose when she let her in at seven thirty.

'Of course not.' And before she could ask if she had spoken to the police yet, Rose opened the door to the lounge.

'I'm glad you could come,' Dennis said, stretching out a hand. It was cold and dry compared to Rose's. 'You remember Paul?'

'Yes. Hello.'

Paul nodded but did not speak. He seemed uncomfortable, for which Rose did not blame him. She should have refused the invitation. Surely tongues would wag when it was known that Dennis had entertained a single woman to dinner only a few days after his wife's death. And it would be known, she was quite sure. Doreen would not be able to keep it to herself. At least Paul was present too.

Dennis poured drinks and between them they managed to fill the half hour until Doreen said the meal was ready with small talk relating mostly to art and Rose's business. 'Dennis,' Rose said, 'I brought some proofs up the other night. Do you know what happened to them?' It was not a tactful question but the police seemed suspicious of her and Dennis had looked at them with his wife.

'No. We chose what we wanted. I assumed you'd taken them with you. The police were asking me about them too.'

They went into the dining-room. Rose let the subject drop.

The house was quiet. Rose had seen the mobile unit outside and wondered if there were actually any men upstairs. Surely by now they would have searched every inch of the place for whatever it was they hoped to find.

The meal was plain but it was hot. Rose's appetite was blunted as she watched her male companions push their food around their plates.

'I'm off now,' Doreen said after she had served the main course. 'There's cheese if you're still hungry.' Rose did not blame her for going to no further trouble. Her efforts would have been wasted.

'Have you made any wedding plans yet?' she asked Paul to try to involve him in the conversation.

'We hadn't, but I spoke to Anna yesterday and we decided there's no point in waiting any longer.'

'Waiting?' It was an odd choice of words. She studied Paul. Straight-nosed, thin-lipped, with soft greyish-blue eyes which did not reflect whatever he might be feeling. His skin was waxen and his hands shook. He was difficult to age but assuming Dennis and Gabrielle were in their early fifties he was probably between twenty-five and thirty.

'Having seen you can never tell what's around the next corner, we thought we might as well go ahead.'

Paul seemed unable to refer to his mother or her death but at least he was making an effort to talk.

'Where will you live?'

'In London. Our work's there and it wouldn't suit us down here. It's too quiet.'

From that statement Rose thought Gabrielle might have left the house to her son rather than her husband.

'As long as Anna's happy, that's all I care about.' For a second there was a flicker of enthusiasm in Paul's manner. It did not last.

'And you, Dennis? Have you made any plans?' Rose was bored with treading around the subject. She had been asked here yet neither man seemed to have noticed she had actually arrived. Perhaps, she thought, Dennis, having been unable to speak to Paul himself, hoped she would break the ice. In which case Gabrielle's name could no longer be ignored. 'I know it's early days yet, but what will you do with Gabrielle's house?'

'I don't know.' He smiled wanly. 'I'm still coming to terms with her not being here. There are problems with my company at the moment, it may be that I'll decide to live here.'

'But you . . .' Paul stopped. There was a tinge of colour across his sharp cheekbones.

His father misunderstood him. 'I wouldn't miss London. I've had my share of the rat-race. If I could get fixed up with something, a lower salary wouldn't bother me. If not,' he wiped his mouth with his serviette, 'well, I'd have to sell and find something smaller. Something like your house, Rose.'

Paul stood up and went over to the table against the wall upon which Doreen had placed cheese, a jug of celery and a basket of biscuits. Rose saw his actions were to hide his feelings, to prevent him saying something he might regret, rather than because he was hungry.

She was right. Paul ate a cube of cheese, then crumbled the biscuit. He filled the silence by saying, 'It might not be yours to sell.'

'What?'

'My mother mentioned to Anna that she might leave us the house.'

Dennis's head jerked up. There was genuine fear in his face. 'When did she tell her that?'

'I'm not sure. Anna only mentioned it recently. It's not a problem, is it?'

Dennis could not believe Gabrielle would have changed her will without telling him. He had to remind himself of Maggie and the things he had not told his wife. 'Paul, you might as well know, it looks as if I'll be made redundant.'

'My God.' He paused. 'But you've still got the flat, that's worth a bit, and they'll pay you off, they'll have to, you've been there years.'

Rose looked from Dennis to Paul, the one so defeated, the other without sympathy. Here was another reason to be grateful she was childless. Paul's parents had brought him up and had, presumably, done what they thought was best for him. Now, when his father most needed support, he showed only callousness. Rose's elbows were on the table, her fingers steepled. Her hands jerked and she knocked her knife to the floor with a clatter. 'I'm sorry,' she said, bending down to pick it up. No, she said silently. No, it can't be. 'It was a lovely meal. I really must go, Dennis.'

He did not try to persuade her to stay longer. Both men stood as she got up; Dennis saw her to the Mini, waited until he was sure it had started, then returned to the house without waving.

Rose was vaguely aware of a light coming from the incident van and the faint purr of a telephone ringing. Although she knew little of police procedure, it crossed her mind that their conversation might have been recorded. So keep out of it, she told herself.

Winding down the window because her face felt hot Rose realised she must be mad to have imagined that Paul had killed his mother in order to inherit, even if his wedding plans had been brought forward. She tried to remember Anna and her first impressions of her, but they had hardly spoken and it would be unfair to judge her when she was in the middle of a row with Paul. Anna was tall and slim and pretty, her straight dark hair cut in a perfect bob, and she knew how to dress, but for some reason Rose did not think she was the type of woman men would kill for. Even from that brief meeting she sensed she lacked personality. However, her views were unimportant, Paul had admitted he would do anything to make Anna happy.

Rose slowed and pulled into a wide spot in the otherwise narrow lane. A car was approaching, headlights on full beam. It did not dawn on her until later that its only destination could be the Miltons' house.

CHAPTER SIX

A dim light filtered into the room through the unlined curtains. Rose had slept well and was comfortable in the double bed, the duvet enveloping her warmly. It had taken a second death to enable her to survive the anniversary of David's without enduring several days of depression. She hated herself at such times but listing all the good things in her life did not help and she gave in to the forces which made it seem each day was grey even when the sun was shining.

She heard the first drops of rain pattering on the window and decided to make coffee and bring it back to bed. I'll take the day off, she thought, read and slop around. I might even light a fire later.

But it was not to be. As she waited for the kettle to boil there was a tap on the window of the kitchen door. She opened it and a draught scattered the sheets of paper upon which she had jotted some notes the previous evening. Laura stood inside the door, her curls bejewelled with raindrops, her clothes dripping water on to the floor and an expression of abject misery on her face.

'Whatever's the matter?'

'Oh, Rose.' The tears came suddenly and rolled down her face. 'It's Trevor,' she said.

'Trevor?'

Rose froze. Had there been an accident? Had his boat gone down?

'We can't stop rowing. Every time he comes home I try so hard to make everything right, nice meals, you know. It's partly my fault, he can't say anything right.' Laura sat at the table. 'Then as soon as he's gone back I feel awful. He's gone off this morning after a blazing row and I keep thinking, if anything happened to him.' She stopped, not wishing to tempt fate.

'He'll ring you later,' Rose told her. 'He always does.' It was true. Each night he was at sea Trevor rang at an arranged time.

'I know. And I'll apologise. But how do I stop it?'

Rose had been aware that things were not quite right but this was the first time Laura had told her. A weight lifted from her shoulders, one she had been unaware of, a minor form of the depression she dreaded. She had been lucky. She and David had had all those months to say all the things that needed saying, to know where they stood with each other. But Rose could not offer the consoling platitude that nothing was going to happen to Trevor. The sea chose its victims randomly.

'And what makes it worse', Laura continued as she accepted the coffee Rose placed before her, 'is that he keeps saying it's my age. It's so bloody insulting. It's his answer for everything.'

'Well, is it?'

'Is it what?'

'Your age? The menopause?'

Laura looked up and smiled faintly. 'I suppose it could be. God, that would make the bastard right. No, it's more than that. He comes in and has a few drinks and he's tired and doesn't want sex, then I get annoyed and we argue. Do you know what he said this morning? He said I sounded like a fishwife. Rose, don't laugh.'

'I'm sorry. He probably didn't see the irony. He *is* a fisherman. Come on, don't sulk. We'll have some more coffee.'

Laura heaped in three spoonfuls of sugar, a sure sign she was upset. 'I'll have to keep trying, I suppose. Anyway, what's all this?'

It was one of Laura's less endearing qualities that once she had poured out her troubles she let other people worry about them, regardless of the effect it had, and was herself able to continue as if nothing had happened. In brightly patterned leggings, a T-shirt and a loose top, her hair curling more tightly because of its soaking, she now looked perfectly cheerful.

'Ah. Just some scribblings.'

'But this is all to do with Mrs Milton's murder.'

Rose chewed her lip as she gently took the paper from Laura's hand. On it she had written what Doreen Clarke had told her as well as everything else which had occurred to her. She would not, not even to Laura, break Doreen's confidence.

'I get it, you're trying to outwit Jacko. He fancies you, you know.'

'What on earth are you talking about?'

'Jack Pearce. It's obvious. I could see by the way he was looking at you.'

'Honestly, Laura, the things you think up.'

Laura grinned and held out her mug. 'Any chance of another, or are you busy? Anyway, what's our Barry going to say about it? Detectives and widowers vying for your favours.' Rose had mentioned the invitation to the Miltons' in a telephone conversation.

Trevor's right, Rose thought later. She's obviously going through some hormonal changes if she believes DI Pearce has anything other than a professional interest in me. And she knew she ought to go and see him.

If she had to go to Camborne – and she certainly wasn't going to present herself at the mobile incident unit in the grounds of the Milton house – then she might as well take her sketching things in case it decided to clear up. The disused mine-stacks, seen from the A30, had frequently been depicted in oils and pastels and sketches but to Rose they were displayed at their best in winter, outlined with low cloud, their crumbling brick stark against bracken and gorse. More than once Rose had felt a sense of utter isolation when working near one of them despite the hum of traffic, and even on the brightest of days she had experienced the hair standing up on the nape of her neck. It lasted only seconds until she heard the sound of a lorry grinding its gears or a crow, its black wings gleaming blue, cawed. Rose never questioned whether this was the product of an over-imaginative brain or whether such things as spirits existed. It was part of life there and she accepted it.

'I don't believe it.' She had picked up an oilskin, one appropriated from Trevor some years ago and never returned, and had her hand on the kitchen door handle when the telephone rang. The answering machine was switched on but Rose was not able to leave it to do its job if she was in the house.

'Do you fancy coming over for something to eat tonight? I've got a rep coming to the shop at six, but any time after seven thirty.'

'Thanks, Barry,' Rose answered guiltily, having mentally gone through the contents of the fridge. It would save shopping.

The fish market was packing up as Rose drove past. She waved to several of the men she had met through Trevor and Laura and who recognised her car. By the time she reached Penzance station the rain had eased and she put the wipers on half-speed, noticing the smears of salty grease on the windscreen.

* * *

Maggie Anderson had decided to front it out. Why leave Dennis with an opportunity to extract himself? He could use many excuses for not seeing her, for not returning to London for some time. It was a double risk under the circumstances but she felt sure she could handle the police, if necessary. The advertising agency had allowed her three days' compassionate leave; she had said there had been a death but did not qualify the statement. As none of her clients was clamouring for attention, and as she did not allow anyone to get close enough to know her family background, what she said was accepted without comment.

Maggie had been more than surprised to see the temporary hut-like structure in front of the house but not as surprised as she was at the reception she received.

I should've phoned, Rose thought as she asked if she could leave the car where it was until she returned. She had expected DI Pearce to be seated behind a desk, which was, she knew, unreasonable. But he was over at Gwithian and would be returning within the hour. Rose was quite firm when she was asked if anyone else could help her and said it was the inspector she needed to speak to. Why? she asked herself, but could not come up with an answer.

Camborne, a granite-built town, dour and uncompromising, was bleaker still in the light drizzle which showed no signs of stopping. Recession-hit, many shops were boarded over and if it wasn't for South

Crofty, the last working tin mine, she did not know how it or Redruth, the neighbouring, almost adjoining town, would survive. But South Crofty had been saved from closure by the injection of capital from a Canadian company and by local, individual investment.

She could have shopped but instead took refuge in Tyacks, a central hotel in Commercial Street, where she ordered coffee. It was brought on a tray by a cheerful waitress. As Rose looked up to thank her, her mouth dropped open in astonishment. In the doorway, shaking an umbrella, was the auburn-haired woman she had seen at the party. She must have been mistaken in thinking it was one of Dennis's friends from London and could not remember why she had had that impression.

The woman walked towards her, pausing for a second before going on to the bar. Rose was not sure if she had been recognised or not. Turning slightly in her seat she waited until the woman had been served then, as she made her way to a table, said, 'Excuse me. Haven't I seen you before somewhere? Were you at the Miltons' party?' Close up, Rose saw fine lines in the translucent skin radiating from the eyes, under which were dark smudges.

'Yes.' Maggie hesitated, unsure if she wanted to become involved in conversation. She had a lot to think about. Finally, having decided that Rose might be an asset to her plans, she asked if she might join her.

'Of course.'

'Maggie Anderson,' she said.

'Rose Trevelyan.'

'Ah, yes. I heard someone mention you. You're the painter, aren't you?'

The painter. It made her sound more important than she was. 'I do paint, yes, but mostly I do photographic work these days. That's how I met Gabrielle.'

'The poor woman. I couldn't believe it. I mean, I'd never even met her before that night. I'm a friend of Dennis's,' she added quickly. 'We met through work.'

'Have the police made you stay down here?'

'No. I . . . well, I didn't like to think of Dennis being left on his own. I was due some leave so I took a few days off.'

To Rose it sounded like a well-rehearsed speech. 'But Paul's there.'

'I didn't know that. I thought he'd go back to London with Anna.'

So Maggie knew enough about the Milton family to realise Paul was capable of being that selfish, of leaving his father alone. Had Dennis told her? 'It seems,' Maggie said honestly, but with some anger, 'that my presence is not required. I stayed here last night. I was going back first thing this morning.'

Rose did not ask why she had changed her mind, she could read the answer in her face. Maggie wanted Dennis and was not going to give him up easily. But how could such a relationship last? One which had begun before Gabrielle's murder? There would be too many painful memories, at least for Dennis, and a constant reminder of his guilt. 'Can I get you another drink?' Rose glanced at her watch. There was time, before she returned to the police station. Let DI Pearce think what he liked if he smelt alcohol on her breath. She would be under the limit if he chose to query it.

'Thank you. A gin and tonic, please.'

Rose ordered a half of bitter for herself and paid the barman. The same waitress was placing a plate of sandwiches on the table. 'I don't know why I ordered this, I'm not hungry.' Maggie stared at the food. 'You've guessed, haven't you?'

'Yes.'

'I always hoped Dennis would get a divorce. His wife had moved down here, I assumed it was because they weren't happy together. I thought I could talk him round in the end. There's nothing I wouldn't . . .' She stopped and picked up a sandwich.

'Do the police know? About you and Dennis?'

'If they do, I didn't tell them. What difference would it make?'

What difference would it make? Rose wondered if Maggie was stupid. 'Did Dennis invite you to the party?' She was beginning to form an assessment of Maggie Anderson's character. It was not a pleasant one.

'No. I wanted to see what his wife was like. He could hardly make a fuss once I was there. And she seemed to accept it. That's not true.' Maggie had seen the expression on Rose's face and had guessed what she must be thinking of her. 'Gabrielle invited me.'

'Gabrielle?'

'She knew. I think she knew from the start. I don't know how she found out – I expect she had enough contacts to make the right inquiries. Unless Paul told her.'

'Paul knew too?'

'We bumped into him by accident once.'

Rose found all this new information hard to assimilate. 'But why would Gabrielle ask you down?'

Maggie smiled for the first time and Rose saw her attraction. 'You obviously don't play the same games, Rose. Think about it. There is Gabrielle as the hostess, in her own home, with her husband. My being there would show the affair up as shabby compared with what Dennis already had. His guilt and fear and anger at seeing me there would be enough for him to end it. Gabrielle was not going to let go, you see.'

Rose felt sick. Did many people carry on in this way? She decided to drop her own bombshell. 'Did you know Dennis is about to be made redundant?'

'What?'

'He told me the other night. When I was having dinner with him.'

Maggie's face reddened but whether it was from anger or some other emotion was not clear.

'Look, I'm sorry, but I've got to go. I've got an appointment.' Rose would have liked to stay longer, but Maggie now knew her name. If, for any unlikely reason, she wanted to speak to her she could look the number up in the book. She was not going to get involved further.

My God, Rose thought as she went out into the cool air. Maggie? Had she realised that evening that she stood no chance, and had she decided to wipe out the opposition? Leave it to the police, her subconscious told her.

'Have a seat, Mrs Trevelyan.' DI Pearce was smiling and polite, perhaps deliberately in contrast to the way she had treated him in her own home. 'Tea or coffee?' Rose shook her head. 'Well, what can I do for you?' Jack Pearce leant back in his chair, relaxed and easy, his hands resting on his lap.

'I . . . well, it sounds daft, but this . . .' She slid a copy of the photograph across the desk.

Jack glanced at it for less than a second, then raised his eyebrows inquiringly.

'Can't you see it?' Rose leant over and pointed to the blur.

'Hmm. Just like in the film.'

'The film? You mean the negative.'

'No. The film. *Blow Up*, I think it was called. You must remember it.'

Was that a deliberate insult? She would have to find out when it was released. She and David had not been great cinema-goers but she often went with Laura now. 'I think that blur might be part of a woman, someone that Mrs Milton did not realise was there.' It was said with cool dignity.

'Could be. Probably Eileen Penrose.'

'Oh.' Rose could think of nothing further to say and she was not going to apologise for doubting the efficiency of the police.

Jack Pearce studied the woman in front of him. She had not, he thought wryly, dressed for the occasion; a yellow T-shirt, faded jeans and a denim jacket were more suitable attire for the cells. Her hair was twisted up and held in place with a tortoiseshell clip resembling a buckle and her pleasant, no, let's face it, he admitted, attractive face looked tired.

'You know.'

'Yes. Several sources told us Mrs Penrose was in the habit of following her husband. He himself admitted he had heard she was up at the house that day, and the lady in question has held up her hand.' He did not add that there was still the matter of her absence around the time Gabrielle was killed. That was not Rose's business.

Rose swallowed. She might as well go the whole way no matter what sort of fool she appeared. 'There's something else which I'm sure you're also already aware of.' It was harder than she had anticipated, this running to the police with tales, and it made her feel disloyal, although to whom she wasn't sure. 'I've been speaking to a lady named Maggie Anderson.'

'And?'

'She and Dennis Milton were having an affair.' No village gossip could have felt worse than Rose did at that moment. She sensed the colour rise into her face.

'You know Miss Anderson?'

'No.'

'Then how come she thought fit to confide in you?'

'I don't know. I met her by chance and we started talking.'

'Before the night of the party?'

'Oh, no. I don't think I even heard her name that evening. Today, I meant.'

'Today?'

Rose felt a moment's satisfaction. Pearce did not know she was back. 'She's staying at Tyacks.'

Jack Pearce tapped the desk with the end of a biro, his mind elsewhere. He had not known about the affair although there had been speculation. Miss Anderson's background had been checked and it was true that the firm Milton worked for had once used the agency's services. Having questioned Milton in depth he was certain he had had no intention of leaving his wife but he had not broken down and confessed to his adultery. Why? To protect himself or his wife's memory, or even the other woman? Or was there a more worrying reason? Rose Trevelyan had been far more helpful than she would ever know but what she had told him was no more than hearsay, if it was true. Anderson may have lied to her for some reason of her own, perhaps to make her jealous. Mrs Trevelyan had, after all, been to the Milton place for dinner.

'Anything else, Mrs Trevelyan?'

'No.' She saw him lean forward and open the top drawer of his desk, stare at something for a second or two, then seem to change his mind. He slid the drawer shut and stood up in one motion, his body, in the small room, appearing taller and better muscled than she remembered it to be. He ran a hand through his dark hair as he held the door open.

'Goodbye.'

'Bye,' Rose said, unable to help seeing his face. He was laughing at her and not doing a very good job of disguising it. 'The bastard,' she hissed as she left the building.

CHAPTER SEVEN

'Did I do the right thing by telling her, Cyril?'

'Leave it, Doreen. That's the third time you've asked me. You've done it, you can't change that.'

'But supposing I was wrong?'

'How can you be? You told me at the time what you'd seen.' Cyril gazed anxiously out of the window, eager to be outside or, failing that, in the greenhouse, not that there was much to do at this time of year. Once the rain starts in these parts, he was thinking, it can go on for weeks.

'I didn't sleep a wink last night, worrying about it.'

Cyril ignored this exaggeration, realising that the real problem was not what she had told Rose Trevelyan: Eileen's antics were known to everyone. It was the thought that the job might be coming to an end and so far she had not had any luck in finding a replacement. 'Do you need any veg, love?'

'No, I don't think so. I might even start on the chutney this afternoon. What time do you want dinner?'

'Oneish.'

Doreen started chopping the tomatoes. Dinner, to her, was the midday meal. Up at the house they ate it in the evening but she always kept the two vocabularies separate. Toilet and lavatory, lounge and front room, napkins and serviettes. Still, she thought, each to their own. Her mind was a storehouse of clichés.

At least she had done her bit and saved Mrs Trevelyan from more bother.

Jim Penrose had had more than enough. He slammed out of the house without touching the food Eileen had prepared for him. It was no good arguing, he always lost. He had never met anyone as expert as his wife at making the smallest omission or the slightest grievance sound like a major crime. Why he stayed with her was beyond him and if everything he did upset her so much, the reverse was also true.

He returned to work, having decided he would not go straight home when he had finished. 'I'll give her something to think about,' he said, his anger mounting when the van refused to start until several attempts later.

'Did you drive here?'

'No, I got the bus most of the way.' Rose shook out her jacket and hung it over the door knob.

'I didn't realise it was raining that hard again.' Barry turned back to the saucepan in which he was stirring something.

'What're we having?'

'Pasta. With my own special sauce.'

'How unusual.'

'Don't be ungrateful, woman. You know it's one of the few things I don't ruin.' He pushed his glasses up, unheedful of the steam which had rendered them useless. 'And if you're rude to the chef, you won't get any wine. You may as well open it, I'm sure you're ready for some.'

Whilst the sauce simmered they sat on the two unmatching chairs either side of the formica-topped table. Barry made enough money for somewhere better but claimed his surroundings didn't bother him. The flat was small enough for him to manage, but to Rose it seemed cramped and inconvenient.

'What's in there?'

Rose had produced an A4 envelope from her bag. 'Just some notes. Tell me what you think.'

Barry saw immediately what she was up to. His instinct was to tell her to stop at once, to leave things to the relevant people, but it might be that she was trying to exorcise a ghost, David's ghost, by facing another sort of death. If she did, would he have a chance?

Rose waited for the verdict. Now she was warm and dry and sipping Barry's wine, which was always superior to what she bought, she began to relax again, forgetting the humiliation Jack Pearce had inflicted upon her. Barry stopped reading once, to place a large pan of water on the cooker to boil, then again to ease in several handfuls of spaghetti.

Rose watched his serious face as he continued to read. The flat was at the back of a building, the only sounds the plopping of the boiling water and a dripping tap, both of which were restful. Condensation covered the windows and the room was aromatic with garlic and tomatoes and the faint smell of soap powder from Barry's shirts which were drying on an old-fashioned wooden pulley strung from the ceiling.

'You're in the wrong trade,' he said at last, jumping up as he remembered the spaghetti. 'You should've joined the police.' He was thoughtful as he strained the pasta. That bit about the trains, it fitted. If it had been someone from Gabrielle's circle in London they would have needed to arrive and depart by car. No trains left the area that late at night and a taxi was out of the question. How could the person, assuming the murder was premeditated, have asked a taxi to wait? It was a ridiculous idea. Nor could one have been called – someone would have remembered if a guest departed early. Besides, as Rose had noted, everyone, according to what she had overheard that night, who was on the guest list was still present when the police arrived. She had ruled out someone on foot; they would have been conspicuous on the narrow lanes, and no one in their right mind would be walking over the cliffs and dunes at night. So, she had concluded, it had to be one of the guests.

They ate in silence for several minutes. Rose was hungry, she had not eaten all day. First Laura, then Maggie, and by the time she got home from speaking to Inspector Pearce she had gone past wanting anything. 'It's excellent, as always.'

'Thanks.' At moments like that, seeing her smile, he was tempted to ask if Rose would like a live-in chef but Barry knew he would not be able to take the disappointment her reply would cause.

'Have the police been back to see you?' she asked after a few more mouthfuls.

'No. Should they have?'

'I don't know. I suppose it means they don't consider you to be a suspect.' She had not told him they had been to see her and did not want to discuss it now.

'Rosie, do you think you know who might have done it?'

'I'm not sure.' She looked down. David used to call her Rosie. Barry did so now occasionally but she didn't have the heart to tell him not to.

'Here, your glass is empty. Did I mention that I'm going to London soon?'

'No. Trade fair?'

'Yes. And if it's all right with you, I'm taking some of your work.' Barry's firm, small as it was, also supplied other outlets. Soon, he realised, he would need to take on a couple more staff. He liked things as they were; expansion scared him and he knew he would not have survived in a city. 'Want to come with me?' he asked casually as he cleared away the plates.

Rose calculated quickly. She was as up to date as she was ever likely to be. 'I'd love to,' she answered. But she hated herself when she saw his face light up. She had her own reasons for wanting to go.

'I'm glad,' Rose said when Laura, during their daily telephone conversation, told her she had spoken to Trevor.

'He was a bit cool, but I don't think I've driven him away completely yet.'

Rose told her about the trip to London. 'With Barry? Is that wise? He might get the wrong idea.'

'No. He went out of his way to let me know he had booked separate rooms.'

'Oh, Rose, I wish we could turn the clock back. We used to have such fun, the four of us.'

'I wish we could too.' But she was not in the mood for Laura's reminiscences. Laura still had a husband. Just. But life had been fun. It was an element which was missing from Rose's present existence.

Replacing the receiver, she was on her way back to the kitchen when her plans were disturbed once more. This time, with the sun behind him, Rose recognised the shape of DI Pearce through the dimpled glass of the front door. 'Yes?' she said abruptly, wishing she didn't look such a mess every time he saw her.

'May I come in?' He followed her into the kitchen and conspicuously eyed the filter machine through which coffee dripped slowly.

He had been polite to her and offered her a drink. 'Would you like coffee?' she heard herself saying ungraciously.

'Love some.'

Rose's mouth was a grim line as she got out milk and sugar. She had intended having half an hour with the paper before setting off for her first appointment of the day.

Jack Pearce leant against the worktop, arms folded, legs crossed at the ankles, as relaxed, apparently, here as he was in his own office. He was in jeans, a blue and white striped shirt and a grey leather jacket. The uniform of the CID as it appeared on television, Rose thought sneeringly, allowing that it did suit him.

'We were concerned about those photographs you took, Mrs Trevelyan, for the very reason you came to see us. We thought they might contain something incriminating and had therefore been stolen. However, there was an innocent explanation for their disappearance. Here.' He handed her the envelope. 'Mrs Clarke had taken them home with her. She thought they would be an upsetting reminder for Mr Milton.'

Rose was pouring milk into the coffee. She turned to look at him, her head on one side. Doreen had not mentioned it to her. 'And she's just remembered and handed them in?'

DI Pearce ignored the question. Rose guessed they had already been in his possession the previous day. Was that what he had been deciding when he looked in his drawer? So why the visit now? 'Thank you. I don't know what I'll do with them. I don't suppose Dennis will want them now. Sit down,' she added belatedly. But Jack Pearce, it seemed, preferred to stand.

He sipped his coffee and asked if she minded if he smoked. She found a blue glass ashtray with the Courage Brewery logo and placed it on the worktop beside him. He glanced at it with a wry grin.

'It was left here by the previous occupants,' she said, annoyed that she felt she had to make an excuse. If he wanted to think she was in the habit of nicking things from pubs, let him.

'Mrs Trevelyan, you seem to be taking quite an interest in this case. Have you now got any ideas as to who might have killed Mrs Milton?'

'No.' She was surprised at the question but she did not know DI Pearce was aware that she was the type of person people confided in and that she might actually know more than she thought she did. Her answer was not strictly honest; she was beginning to have a vague idea but it was based on instinct rather than elimination or facts.

'Ah, well. I'd better be going. Thanks for the coffee.'

Rose noticed he had left half a mugful as he let himself out through the kitchen door.

There was just time to hang out the washing that had been in the machine overnight. She was taking a chance but it didn't look like rain at the moment. Her first assignment was a portrait for a local writer whose publisher required a new picture for the jackets of his books. It was straightforward work: a few shots in his own home. She made sure she had the background sheet which folded down to nothing in its metal frame. It would not be worth coming back again because at twelve thirty she was due at the offices of a firm of solicitors where one of the partners was retiring. He had been with the firm for thirty years and a surprise party was being held during the lunchtime. She was to take a photograph of the presentation of whatever it was they had decided to give him.

The author was charming and did not interfere or make suggestions. Rose told him he could expect the proofs in a week to ten days' time, then left his terraced house. Because they had been chatting, Rose asking questions about his books, she had only half an hour to kill. She might as well get there early and be prepared.

There was space for the car in the firm's small car park. Taking her equipment with her, she asked the receptionist which room was to be used for the presentation. 'In there, the senior partner's office.' She pointed to a door across the passage. 'It's all right, you can go in. They're just laying out the food.'

Rose introduced herself and was handed a glass of wine. A cold buffet had been set out on a white sheet covering the large desk. She shuddered, recalling the last buffet she had attended.

Finally most of the staff were assembled and a smiling man was led in by a secretary. Rose captured his expression as the door opened but guessed, by how hard he tried to look surprised, that he could not have missed all the activity that had been going on during the morning.

She took two shots of the wrapped gift being handed to him by the senior partner and another of the retiring man holding the gift box open. It contained a carved wooden pipe rack and two expensive-looking pipes and, by the smile on his face when he opened it, the contents would give him far more pleasure than the ubiquitous clock.

'One more, please.' The senior partner paused. 'Ready?'

Rose nodded and focused on the two men. This time an envelope was involved but she did not get to see the amount written on the cheque it contained.

She was duly thanked and left with the rest of the day free. There were two exposures left on the roll of film; she would, as she often did, waste them. Rose tried to keep one job to one film but today, each client needing so few shots, she had used the same one.

The sky over Newlyn was darker, grey clouds banking up behind the houses built in the side of the hill. With luck she would get back before it rained and if the washing was dry she would iron it.

Maggie Anderson did not want to cut her losses but if she stayed she would antagonise Dennis further. His reaction to her arrival was violent. 'How dare you?' he had shouted when Paul had shown her in. She had not been allowed the chance to explain that her invitation to the party had been issued by Gabrielle, that she had not gate-crashed. But why should he believe it? She had not mentioned it in London. She had kept the invitation, it was still in her handbag, and it stayed there because, before she could utter another word, Dennis had gripped her by the elbow and virtually thrown her out of the house.

Later, after her encounter with Rose, Maggie had telephoned the house and left a message with the housekeeper to say where she was staying, asking Dennis to ring her. He had not returned the call and, after a second night in the hotel, Maggie knew there was no alternative but to return to London.

She paid her bill, her face gaunt, her auburn hair dull. The loose-cut trousers and blouse which hung perfectly could not make her attractive after two nights without sleep. She threw on an olive raincoat, picked up her holdall and left, unaware that an hour later Inspector Pearce came looking for her.

Once on the M5 she settled into the driving. The conditions were good; no rain to cause spray, no sun slanting at an awkward angle. The greyness overhead suited her mood. She felt bad about Rose Trevelyan; she had been arrogant in her company, behaved badly, and the woman did not deserve it. She had been the one to find the body and had probably not recovered from the shock. But why had Dennis had her to dinner? Surely he wasn't deceiving Maggie the way he had his wife? She couldn't leave it alone. She must find out.

The Cornwall she had left behind was drab and dreary, so different from the warmth of her arrival. She did not want to go back again. London was the place for her with its theatres and cinemas and restaurants and shops, where it didn't matter if it rained.

'Yes,' Jim Penrose had admitted when Eileen placed his midday meal in front of him. 'I went up there a third time. I don't know why you're making such a fuss. Mrs Milton simply wanted me to show her where the stopcock was. It was well hidden, it wasn't an excuse. Besides, I've told the police all this. Anyone'd think you suspected me. You've got more reason than me for killing her, with your nasty, jealous ways.'

'You can't deceive me, Jim Penrose.'

'The woman's dead. Let it be.'

'Attractive, wasn't she, with all that black hair? And you, touching her arm like . . .' Eileen had stopped, knowing she had gone too far.

'Touching her arm? When?' Realisation dawned. 'You bitch, you've been following me.'

116

Eileen turned away and busied herself at the sink. That was when he had walked out. If she had gone to those lengths, was she capable of murder? He could not bear to think of it. But the police had been back again to see her. She had not said so but he had seen them drive off as he returned the previous evening. His own interview had gone on long enough but he understood the reason. He had been on the premises three times and knew his way around. His wife was working there on the night of the party and would be otherwise occupied; if he had reason to kill Mrs Milton it was a perfect opportunity, especially as no one would be surprised to see him with Eileen being there. Mrs Milton had mentioned the party to him and, although she had phrased it subtly, he understood why he was not to be a guest. It might lead to awkwardness between husband and wife if one was present in a social capacity and the other as an employee. Had Gabrielle also had an inkling of Eileen's suspicions? If so, she had definitely done the right thing. Eileen would never have forgiven him if he had accepted an invitation.

After he had installed a shower unit in a newly converted cottage it was still only four thirty, and Jim had no more work that day. He left the van quite close to the house, handy for the morning, then took himself to the nearest pub. He did not intend his drinking to be limited by what Eileen thought was good for him, nor would he be home in time for the supper which was always on the table at six thirty.

And, he thought defiantly, I shan't go home until she's back from Bingo. That'll give her something to think about. Jim Penrose ordered his second pint of Hicks bitter.

Satisfied that the clothing she had chosen as suitable for London was ironed and in the airing cupboard, Rose wondered exactly how she would go about what she planned to do. Barry had telephoned to say he would pick her up at ten so they could reach London in time to shower and change and have a couple of drinks before dinner. The trade show was not until the day after. Barry would attend for all of the first day but only the morning of the second. It was all over by then anyway, and most of the stalls started packing up around lunchtime.

Still not having shopped, Rose drove down to Newlyn and got a Chinese takeaway. It would also save washing up and she would, no matter who tried to interrupt her, have an evening at home with a book.

Only half her mind was on the radio programme she had switched on to listen to whilst she ate. Presumably the police had spoken to everyone who had been at the Miltons' that night but they didn't seem to be getting anywhere. Not that they would tell me, Rose reflected. And presumably, if more questions needed to be asked of the few people from London, the Met would deal with it.

* * *

Barry was exactly on time and Rose was ready. For the journey she was wearing trousers; her tan suit was carefully folded in her overnight bag. 'I'm looking forward to this,' she said. And she was.

The prospect of two days away from work and all that had been happening was a welcome one. She would, of course, be pleased to come home again when it was over.

'Are you coming to the fair with me?'

'Not the first day. I want to do some shopping.' Of a sort, she added silently, still unsure why she was so obsessed with Gabrielle Milton's death. Perhaps it was because she had found the body and because she felt she had lost a possible friend. 'Do you know, this is the first time I've been up since David died?'

Barry glanced at her briefly, then returned his eyes to the road. It was not said with any trace of pain.

With a shock Rose realised how parochial she had allowed her life to become.

Barry took one hand off the wheel to brush back the strands of hair over his balding scalp. He had timed it well, the roads were not too busy at this hour. But shopping? In the twenty-odd years he had known Rose she had never shown the least interest in shopping. It crossed his mind she might want to purchase new clothes to impress Dennis Milton.

Rose was also thinking of Dennis. If her efforts came to nothing she would invite him over, with Paul and Anna. Paul had said she would be down again for the weekend. And what was it that Paul did that allowed him so much time off work? At dinner, Dennis had said he was staying down at least another week. Strange she had not thought to ask, she was naturally curious.

'Do you want me to drive?' Rose asked when they stopped at Exeter services for petrol and a cup of coffee.

'Think you can handle it?'

Rose narrowed her eyes. 'I've driven bigger and better cars than yours.'

'Only teasing.'

Rose took the wheel and switched on the radio. It was tuned to Radio 4. She fiddled with the knob and found a music station. She was in the mood for something livelier.

They had taken it steadily and, with the stop, reached London a little after five o'clock. The hotel had an underground car park with a complicated security system which they finally worked out. Having registered at the desk they went up to their separate rooms. 'See you in the bar at – what? Seven? Is that too early?'

'That's fine, Barry.'

'You don't want to do any shopping first?'

'They close at five thirty!'

'I appreciate that, Rosie, dear, but I suspect it's not retail shopping you were talking about.'

'I . . .' But Barry was already striding down the corridor, turning once to smirk at her over his shoulder.

She was downstairs first and sat at the bar on a stool, absent-mindedly picking at the peanuts and olives in dishes in front of her. Showered, her hair pinned up neatly, and dressed in the tan suit, a cream shirt and heeled shoes, she had thought she would blend in with the other clientele; however, some of the women strolling through the marbled reception area, which she could see through the wide doorway, and those who entered the bar with their escorts, made her feel provincial. Suddenly she grinned. The barman smiled back and asked if she wanted another drink.

'No, thanks.' It had occurred to her, perched as she was in full view, a single female with her slim legs crossed, that she might be sending out all the wrong signals. Two businessmen came in, briefcases in hand, but they did not give her a second glance. Rose was not sure whether to be pleased or disappointed.

'Been waiting long?' Barry asked.

'No. Ten minutes.'

'Sorry. Had to make a couple of calls. What're you drinking?'

'Vodka and tonic. I didn't want to get stuck into the cocktails.'

'Have what you like, it's all going on the bill.'

'I'm paying for myself, Barry.'

The barman watched with amusement as they argued amiably about how they would settle the account. Rose finally convinced Barry that she was not prepared to let him pay but agreed the drinks could go on his room. At times like that she saw why a relationship, other than the one they had, would not have worked. Barry could be peevish at times, almost petulant, like a small child, and she became exasperated with him. He pushed his glasses firmly on to the bridge of his nose and turned away, not speaking for several minutes.

'Where shall we go to eat?'

They had glanced in at the hotel dining-room and studied the menu on the board outside but it did not appeal to them. Rose would let him pay for the meal; she did not want any more sulking.

Enjoying the sights and sounds they strolled around and found a restaurant which they both liked. When they returned to the hotel Rose fell asleep immediately.

'Come on the train, Anna, there's no point in us having both cars here. I'll pick you up from the station.' Paul had studied the timetable Gabrielle kept handy. 'I love you,' he said, once the arrangements were made.

'Me too,' Anna replied. She replaced the receiver. With Gabrielle dead everything had changed. Paul had been fond of his mother, more than fond, unlike the way she had felt about her own parents. She had never been able to forgive them for what she thought of as their sins. She had not seen them for ten years.

Anna picked up the telephone again, dialled the number of the shop where her wedding dress was being made and arranged a time for a fitting.

At the weekend she would return to Cornwall and take stock of exactly how much Paul had inherited. It had taken her a long time to come this far.

* * *

Rose and Barry breakfasted early as Barry was due at the exhibition centre at eight thirty to get set up. 'Shall we meet back here?'

'Yes. That's easiest. About the same time? And it's my turn to pay for the meal tonight.' Rose had agreed he could pay for her room, otherwise she would never hear the end of it, but she would not allow him to pay for everything. Barry did not have time to argue.

Hoping she appeared more confident than she felt, Rose got a Tube to the area where the music company Dennis worked for was based. She found it easily and made her request to the receptionist, expecting to be asked a lot of questions or to have to see someone else. She held her breath as the girl put through a couple of incoming calls. She had got the address from Yellow Pages having remembered the name from the night of the party when Gabrielle mentioned it as they were going through the proofs. It was a company even Rose had heard of.

'Thank you, that's very kind.' Rose left the building without having to speak to anyone else. How easily she had lied and how quickly the girl had believed her. Rose had told her she was an old friend of the Miltons and had only just heard the news. She pretended to be disappointed to hear Dennis was not in the office.

'I'm not sure where he is. All I know is that he won't be back for a while yet.'

'Oh dear,' Rose had said. 'I've tried their address in Cornwall and he's not there either.'

Without having to ask, she was provided with the number and street of the London flat. The girl, presumably, thought that if Rose knew the Miltons well enough to possess one address there could be no harm in letting her have the other.

What do I expect to find there? she thought as she waited to cross the busy street. Studying the Tube map she saw the journey only involved one change.

Luck was with her. The woman who cleaned for Dennis answered the door. 'I'm only here twice a week at the moment,' she said, asking Rose in. 'Just to keep an eye on the place really. I still can't take it in, you know. Such a lovely woman.' She stopped and studied Rose suspiciously. 'We haven't met before, have we?'

'No. I've been away for quite a long time. I've only just heard myself. I thought Dennis might be here, they said at his office they weren't sure where he was.'

'He's still down there. I don't know what he'll do about the funeral.'

'Well, I'm sorry to have troubled you. Perhaps it would have been a bit much for Dennis, me turning up out of the blue. I know . . .' She paused as if the idea had just come to her. 'I could get a message to him via Paul. That way, if he doesn't want to see people there's no harm done.' She rummaged in her handbag. 'Damn it I haven't got my diary with me.'

'I can't help you there, dear.' The woman, who had not given her name, sniffed and brushed back stiff blonde hair. 'I don't know where he lives. I know where his office is, though.'

'Fine. I'll leave a message there.'

'You can phone from here if you like. I'm sure Mr Milton wouldn't mind.'

'No, don't worry. I'd prefer to write a note.'

She listened to the directions and memorised them. Wandsworth was not an area she knew. By the time she got there it was almost lunchtime.

Standing outside the run-down premises she thought Dennis's cleaner must have been mistaken, but the sign on the fascia board confirmed that it was the right place. Paint peeled from the woodwork where the sun had blistered it and the window, through which could be seen revolving cards displaying properties, was dirty. It might be that the place was leased and the landlord responsible for outside upkeep, but surely Paul had the money for a coat of paint?

The inside was a little better.

'Can I help you?' A young man jumped up from his seat behind a teak-veneered desk.

'I'm not sure. I'm looking for a flat really, but I wasn't sure where to start.'

'Renting or buying?'

'Renting.' Rose did not want to raise the man's hopes; perhaps he would simply say they did not deal in rented accommodation.

'Actually, we've got a couple of places on the books. I'm not sure they'll be what you're after, though.' He seemed to be sizing her up. 'Of course, if you did decide to buy you wouldn't be wasting all that rent.' He turned and pulled open the drawer of a filing cabinet. 'Are you from around here?' Rose shook her head. 'You do realise how expensive things are in London?' He had detected a West Country burr. 'How many bedrooms were you thinking of?' There was a wedding band on her finger; there might be teenage children.

'Oh, two, I suppose.' How adept she was in deceit, but how mean it made her feel. 'I'm a widow,' she added, just to add some particle of truth.

'I'm sorry.'

'It's all right.' People always said they were sorry. How could they be, when they knew neither her nor David? But the young man was pleasant enough.

'Did you just walk in on the off-chance or did you hear of us through somebody?'

'I was passing, but I had heard of you. One of my friends knows Paul Milton. That's not you, is it?'

'No. Paul's the boss. He's away at the moment. Family problems.'

Rather an understatement, Rose thought, but he might only be aware that Gabrielle was dead, not that she had been murdered. No, impossible. The police would have made their own investigations: if this was the state of Paul's business, he might be more than keen to inherit earlier than was anticipated. She gave the man credit for his circumspection.

'May I take these with me?'

'Of course. I could take you to look at them this afternoon if you like.'

Rose was at the door. 'I'd like to study the details first. I'll let you know.' How ridiculous to imagine she could swan up to London and hope to find anything. Did she really think she was smarter than the Met? Possibly smarter than DI Pearce, though. Pearce with the laconic expression and mocking eyes who never seemed to be in a rush and was surely getting nowhere in finding Gabrielle's killer.

'Mrs, er . . . just a minute.'

Rose was surprised to see the young man in the shop doorway, locking up.

'Look, I haven't been strictly fair with you. It's just . . . well, I feel I may have wasted your time.'

'Oh?' She was not the only one who wasn't playing straight. 'Look, it's almost one. Do you fancy a quick drink and a sandwich?'

'Yes. Why not? There's a good place about a hundred yards down the road.' He turned the sign to closed and locked the door.

They walked in silence, both surprised at the situation they had found themselves in. 'My name's Gareth.'

'I'm Beth.' Rose crossed her fingers. At least it was her mother's name. She did not want Paul or Dennis to find out she'd been snooping.

Rose insisted on paying for the drinks and they took them to a table near the frosted window. A plush bench seat ran along the length of the wall. The tables were solid, with heavy iron legs. It was a typical city pub and filling up rapidly.

The extractor fans were prominent and noisy but had little effect on the stale, heavy air or the cigarette smoke which drifted upwards in spirals. All was overlaid with the smell of chips.

'I don't know what to say really, Beth.'

He was not afraid of using her name. It was probably a good selling technique.

'Beth,' he repeated, causing her to smile. 'It suits you.' He studied her unselfconsciously. When she had been with David she had been pleased to be the object of complimentary glances because she was in a position of being safe and loved. These days, if she received them, she did not notice. What did Gareth make of her from a distance of about twenty years?

'You said you'd heard of us. How well do you know Paul Milton?'

'Not that well at all. Why do you ask?' The positions had been reversed. Rose was supposed to be asking the questions.

'It's just that if you were a friend. No . . . never mind.'

'What's bothering you, Gareth?'

'God, it's awful. I don't know what to do, and now with the police. Look, Paul is the boss in real terms although he persuaded me to go into partnership with him. His share of the business is the greater. To be honest, I was happy enough working for him. I like meeting people and the salary was acceptable. I wasn't going to be an estate agent for ever, I go to night classes. We were doing well and I changed my mind. Then the recession hit. And now . . . well . . .' He left another sentence unfinished.

'And now?'

'I'm not sure.'

Rose guessed he was deciding how much he could tell her without being disloyal but it was obvious he needed someone to talk to. Who better than a stranger whom he would never see again?

'I've been sitting there hour after hour in that bloody empty office and I can't get hold of Paul. There's no answer from his flat and I don't have the number in Cornwall. I'm tempted just to lock up and dump the keys through the letter-box.'

'Are you in some sort of trouble?'

'Yes. Financially, that is. We owe money all over the place. If something isn't done about it within a few days the bailiffs'll be in. Not that there's anything much for them to take. The fax and most of the electronic stuff is on lease. Paul does all the bookwork, you see. I had no idea how deeply we were in, not until the police came to speak to me about Mrs Milton's death and they began looking into Paul's financial status.'

Rose had expected it would be so but she was disappointed to hear it. Did they suspect Paul, then? Perhaps that's why he was still in Cornwall, maybe he had no choice but to remain there until the investigation was over.

'But I thought I'd heard his parents had money, couldn't they have helped him out?'

Gareth shook his head. The mid-brown hair, brushed back and gelled, remained motionless. 'They've bailed him out before. From what I gather they've refused to do so again. At least I haven't got a girlfriend at the moment. Paul's got Anna to think of. They're supposed to be getting married.'

Things were falling into place. No wonder they had brought forward their wedding; Anna did not look the sort to put up with making do. If Gabrielle had left them the house it would sell for a lot of money, enough probably for Paul to start up in something else.

'I was so worried,' Gareth was saying. 'You see, initially, I thought . . . well, I thought Paul may have done it. Killed his mother.'

Only when spoken aloud, and by somebody other than herself, did the enormity of one of the possibilities Rose had been considering hit her.

It was strange how looks and a certain sort of upbringing could lead to misconceptions. Paul dressed and spoke nicely and exuded confidence even though he was not very talkative in her presence. She had put his manner down to grief, not realising how many other worries he had; Paul's careful upbringing had not done him much good.

'Beth? Another drink?'

'Oh, yes, please.' Barry would have been amazed to

know how long she had been sitting nursing an empty glass.

'I'm sorry, I've been boring you. I just wanted you to know that if you had decided on any of those flats I'm not sure that the deal would've gone ahead.'

'Thank you for being honest,' Rose said, knowing what a hypocrite she was.

'Well . . .' He grinned. It was a nice smile. 'You've helped me make up my mind. I'm not going back there. I'll post the keys to Paul's house and write him a letter. As soon as I get another job I'll start repaying whatever my share of the debt is. Thanks for listening. You're a nice lady. You remind me of my mum.'

'Cheers.' Rose raised her glass sardonically. She could have done without the last comment.

The conversation moved on to more general topics, then Rose said she had to leave. There was time, after all, to do some shopping. Maybe a dress which she would wear this evening – that would make Barry eat his words.

'Nice meeting you, Beth.' Gareth shook her hand. 'Poor old Paul, there's nothing he wouldn't do for Anna and I think the reverse is also true. They idolise one another.'

Was it intended, Rose wondered, to be a deliberate parting shot? Was Gareth trying to tell her something? He did, she noticed, walk away in the opposite direction from that in which the shop lay.

As she stood on the pavement orientating herself she recalled what Barry had said about Paul trying to gain his father's attention. Had he been trying to talk Dennis into lending or giving him more money? And, having failed, had he taken things into his own hands? And if he was so devoted to Anna – if, as he claimed, there was nothing he would not do to make her happy – wasn't this another motive? So why had he and Anna been arguing?

The dress was of pale-blue wool, fully lined and so very soft to the touch. Rose saw it and had to have it. She only shook a little as she signed the credit card slip but it flattered her and brought out the colour of her eyes.

Not until she was halfway down Regent Street did she realise she had no shoes to match. The court shoes she had brought to go with the suit were tan.

With a little shrug she returned to Oxford Street to find a shoe shop. It's only money, she thought, and heard the oft-repeated phrase used in West Cornwall for any and every eventuality: 'Madder do er?' It had taken her several weeks to discover this meant 'It doesn't matter, does it?' and only the upward inflection at the end had given it away.

Back at the hotel she had enough time for a soak in the bath, much needed after the grime of the city. The dress was on a hanger, the navy shoes by the bed. She had taken the precaution of rubbing soap around the heels. Her tendency to wear espadrilles or sandals all summer made winter shoes rub initially.

Why, as she soaped herself, Jack Pearce should come into her mind was a mystery, but she saw his face clearly. Ought she to say where she had been? No, there was no need. The police had already spoken to Gareth.

'Wow. Terrific,' was all Barry said when she met him that evening.

Too late Rose realised Barry might believe she was all dressed up for his benefit.

Doreen Clarke, clad in a raincoat and with a woollen hat pulled down over her straight grey hair, got into Cyril's car feeling like a schoolgirl let out early. The Miltons were going out in the evening and she need not return that day.

'Can't make that girl out at all,' she said, strapping the seat belt around her. 'Doesn't say much. Nervy sort, if you ask me. Still, if there's a big wedding coming up it's hardly surprising.'

Cyril waited patiently for traffic to pass before he negotiated the roundabout at the bottom of the hill.

'*He's* all right, Mr Milton – not quite as classy as his wife, but his heart's in the right place. I heard them talking about the will. Seems the solicitor's been on the phone. Apparently they were going to do it proper, like – you know, have it read out after the funeral, though God knows when that'll take place. Seems the police've got there first. They wanted to know what was in it, who'd benefit.'

Cyril waited. He wondered how his wife had been privy to this conversation. It was not the sort of thing discussed in front of the daily. He did not put her in an awkward position by asking.

'Cyril? Aren't you interested?'

'Yes. I was waiting for you to go on.'

'Well, I couldn't hear the rest of it because of all the shouting. All hell was let lose, I can tell you. Do you think they'll put it in the paper? How much she left?'

'I doubt it. They usually only do that when there're no beneficiaries or if one person receives an enormous figure.'

'Well, they might, if it's relevant to the murder. I hope they do.'

Cyril let her continue talking. No doubt Doreen would find out what the sum was through one means or another.

'You won't mind if I go to Bingo, will you?' Doreen had not been for several weeks. Mostly she went with Maureen but since Eileen had started going too, she had taken to going with a neighbour. Maureen was a laugh; she could not understand how two sisters could be so unalike.

'You enjoy yourself, love. You haven't had a night out for ages.'

By his complaisant smile Doreen guessed there would be football on the television.

She rang the neighbour, Teresa, and arranged to call for her. They always had one drink first, a whisky and lime for Doreen, and a bottle of Pils for her friend. After the session, in which Teresa shared a win and picked up four pounds, they returned to the pub. It was much busier now with only half an hour or so before last orders were called. It was Teresa's turn to buy the round.

They watched the other customers, easy in each other's company. A group of men were discussing rugby; there were several couples and a pair in their late teens in the corner. 'Look at them,' Doreen said. 'It's embarrassing to watch. I don't know why they've wasted their money on drink. They might as well go home to bed and get on with it.'

'Doreen!' Teresa laughed and turned to see if she knew who the couple were. 'Jesus! Don't look now, but you'll never guess who's just come in.'

'Who? My, my. Fancy that.' Doreen stared openly at Jim Penrose and Rita Chynoweth as they entered the bar, arm in arm and both, she guessed, the worse for wear.

'Wait till Eileen hears about this. Still, it won't be from me.'

'Nor me,' Doreen said. But she would have liked to be there when Eileen did hear.

Barry was startled when Rose produced a small plastic bag and handed it to him. 'A gift,' she said.

'Isn't it a bit . . . well . . . modern for me?' He held the loudly patterned tie away from him as if it was offensive.

'No. Everyone's wearing them. It'll go with that jacket you got in Burton's sale. You should splash out more, you've nothing else to spend your fortune on.'

I'd spend my money on you, Rosie, he thought. 'Thank you.' He kissed her cheek, which was the only intimacy she ever allowed him. 'Ok. Let's go and eat.' Barry was too moved to add anything further.

'I could get hooked on this.' Rose stirred the cocktail she was drinking.

'You'd get hooked on tap water if someone told you it was alcoholic. You still coming with me tomorrow?'

'Yes.' She had had enough of the Miltons. Her obsession, she realised, was fading. And it would be interesting to see if anyone was keen to buy any of her work in its finished form.

The following day left them both exhausted, and Barry drove off as soon as he had delivered Rose to her door. The trade fair had been busier during the second morning than Barry had anticipated, then there was the packing up and the long drive back.

Rose had looked around the fair but had to admit, after two hours, she was bored. She whiled away the time drinking coffee. They had toyed with the idea of staying a third night and driving back slowly the next day but it would have been unfair on the woman who had come in to run the shop in Barry's absence.

Rose drove for the first part of the journey home and they stopped again at the same services; she was fascinated by the crowds of people and asked Barry where he thought they could all be going. It was warm and they were surrounded with the smell of food. Rose could see how tired Barry was and insisted they drive with the radio on and the windows open.

It was with a sense of relief that she let herself in, threw on the light switches and dumped her holdall on the bottom stair. 'We'll get our priorities right here,' she said aloud, reaching for the corkscrew and a bottle of claret. They had not had a drink as both of them were driving. She carried the glass through to the sitting-room. The light on the answering machine was flashing twice rapidly in succession before a short pause. She clicked it on. 'I don't particularly wish to leave a message,' Laura's voice told her, 'but as your social life's so full lately, I suppose I'll have to. I'll call round in the morning. I want to hear every sordid detail of your two nights in London.'

Rose smiled. Typical Laura. Straight in with what she wanted to say and no clue as to who was calling. Except that, after all those years, Rose could not mistake her voice.

'Mrs Trevelyan,' the second message started. This was a voice she did not know. Rose sat on the chair nearest the telephone with a pen and paper handy. 'It's Maggie Anderson. I'd hoped to catch you at home. It's now six thirty. If it's convenient I'll try again later.'

But six thirty when? Tonight or yesterday? If it had been the previous day Maggie may have got tired of getting nothing but the machine. No, it had to be tonight. Laura knew when she was due back and had said she would see her in the morning. Maggie's call had come after Laura's.

With a second glass of wine beside her, Rose ate some

cheese on toast which was all she was up to making and thought over the events of the last two days. Tomorrow, maybe, she would commit those thoughts to paper.

At eleven thirty she pulled the duvet up around her ears and turned on her side with the intention of reading. When she woke the bedside light was still on and her book was on the floor, pages splayed. Maggie Anderson had not rung back.

Laura did not stay long once she had learnt that Rose and Barry had remained in their separate rooms. Chewing her lip as she wondered if it was wise to invite Dennis to her home, Rose dialled the number anyway. He accepted the invitation on behalf of the three of them, having spoken briefly to Paul – he must have been in the same room for Rose heard a muffled conversation. Anna, who had not yet arrived down from London, was not to be consulted, it seemed.

It was a blustery day, the windows rattled and the first of the falling leaves were swept across the lawn. Rose made coffee and took it up to the darkroom where she developed the film containing the two jobs she had done the previous week. As she worked she planned what she would cook for the Miltons, a task she looked forward to. Apart from the occasional visit from Laura or Barry she had only herself to cater for and, although she ate well, she would enjoy having to make a real effort.

Mid-morning it began raining again. Rose flicked

the switch and the kitchen was bright, the overhead fluorescent light dispelling the shadows. With a dog-eared cookery book open in front of her she made a shopping list. When the phone rang she half expected it to be Dennis, cancelling the arrangement.

'Mrs Trevelyan? It's Maggie Anderson. I'm sorry I didn't get back to you last night. I . . . well, I wanted to apologise. I was rude to you that day in Camborne. I hope you don't mind me ringing.'

'No.' Rose was puzzled. She had known something wasn't quite right when they had that one drink together and it had crossed her mind that the woman might try to contact her. But why? 'I was surprised at what you told me, I didn't think you were particularly rude.'

'I shouldn't have said anything. There was no reason for me to involve you.'

'It's all right. I shan't say anything.' Not to Dennis or his family or anyone else, but she had already told DI Pearce. To have hidden it, she excused herself, might be classed as shielding a suspect. Both Dennis and Maggie might have wished for Gabrielle to be out of the way.

'Thank you. It's too late for that, though. The police came to see me again last night. That's why I was unable to call you back. It's the second time since I've been home.'

During the pause Rose sensed her anxiety. 'Do they suspect you?'

'Yes. But I didn't do it. God, if only I could turn the clock back. I should never have accepted that invitation.

139

And Dennis won't have anything to do with me, I believe he might suspect me too.'

Maggie Anderson was paying for her sins and Rose felt some sympathy. There was little she could say to her, and she was not really sure why Maggie had rung. Why apologise to someone you had spoken to once and you were not likely to come across again? Unless it was a ploy – perhaps Maggie hoped she'd put in a good word for her with Dennis. But Rose was not going to interfere. A bit late for that, she thought, when the conversation had come to a faltering end. Why else had she invited the Miltons over?

When the rain stopped she walked down to the shops and purchased what she would need for the following evening plus staples for the fridge. Not fancying a struggle up the hill with the groceries she stood at the bus stop where several other people were already waiting. When a car she did not recognise tooted, Rose did not, at first, realise that DI Pearce was behind the wheel. He leant across to the passenger side. 'Need a lift?' he asked through the partially opened window.

She hesitated, feeling curious eyes upon her. 'Thank you,' she said coolly and got into the car.

'Home, I take it?'

'Please.' She remained silent, wondering why he was in Newlyn and hoping it was not because he needed to speak to her again.

He pulled in off the road but was unable to get into the drive. His car was too large and Rose's was parked there anyway. 'Do I get invited in for coffee? You do make nice coffee.'

'Really? You left it last time. I do have things to do.' She had imagined his tone was playful.

'I, too, have things to do, Mrs Trevelyan,' he replied, letting her see her mistake. 'I have to find whoever killed Gabrielle Milton. Can you spare me a few minutes?'

'Yes.' It was an official visit then. How stupid of her to have thought otherwise. She tried to ignore her disappointment.

DI Pearce did not offer to carry her shopping. She dumped it on the back doorstep and unlocked the door, leaving him to follow and shut it behind him. Silently she filled the kettle. It would be instant this time.

'Mrs Trevelyan—'

'Oh, for goodness' sake, call me Rose.'

'Rose, then. I asked you before if you knew of anyone who would wish Mrs Milton harm. You assured me you did not. You claim you barely knew the lady. You also claimed you had never set eyes on Miss Anderson before the party either.'

'It's true.' Rose jumped to her own defence. Jack Pearce irritated her.

'All right. But I find it hard to understand, if you have so little interest in the family, why you've been poking around in London, turning up at the Miltons' flat and questioning Paul Milton's partner.'

Rose felt the colour flooding into her face. Put like that, she sounded like an interfering old bag.

'What you told us, about Miss Anderson, has been very helpful but I find it surprising that she confided such a matter to a stranger. Can you enlighten me?'

'No. I don't know why she did it. And she telephoned to apologise for doing so. Perhaps she just wanted to get it off her chest.' Better to admit to the call; the way Pearce was getting at her she wouldn't be surprised if he had tapped her line.

'Possibly. Another possibility is that she thinks you know something; that she is trying to cultivate your friendship in order to find out what it is.'

'You have a nasty mind, inspector.'

'It's a nasty job, Rose. What were you aiming to do? In London?'

'I don't know.' She tightened the band around her hair for something to do with her hands, feeling like a scolded child. 'Maybe you think I killed Gabrielle. Is that why you keep coming here?'

'It crossed my mind.'

She had, she realised, asked for that. Naturally everyone who had attended that evening would be under suspicion. And she had found the body. 'I never went upstairs.'

'Upstairs?'

'She was pushed from the balcony.'

'Was she? Now who told you that?'

'Well, I assumed . . . we all assumed . . .' She stopped, knowing each time she opened her mouth she made herself appear more of a fool in DI Pearce's eyes.

'Assumptions are dangerous things, Rose.' Absent-mindedly he heaped four spoonfuls of sugar into his coffee and stirred it. 'However, I have it on good authority you would not be capable of murder.'

'Oh?'

'Your friend, Laura.' He smiled. 'I bumped into her the other day.' Rose Trevelyan, he thought, is extremely uncomfortable in my presence, but her feelings do not arise out of guilt.

Rose, as if realising the impression she was making, sat down, glad she was wearing a Viyella checked shirt and a newish pair of cords. She was not at quite such a disadvantage as the other times he had seen her. She had forgotten about first impressions, and that Jack Pearce's initial sight of her had been when she was dressed for the party. 'I see. You make a habit of discussing suspects or witnesses with their best friends, do you?' She was furious to think Laura had chatted with him in such a manner.

'We make a habit of speaking to anyone who knows anyone at such times. But if it makes you feel better, it was a chance meeting and your name came into the conversation.'

Rose stood up and began unpacking the groceries, hoping he would take it as a hint to leave. She had not done anything illegal, he must know that.

'You like a drink?' He nodded at the wine rack and at the two bottles she had bought at the Co-op to go with the meal she would cook for the Miltons.

'Is that any of your business as long as I don't go out in the car?' She could not be civil to him. He seemed to fill the kitchen and, always, he seemed to be enjoying a private joke at her expense.

'No offence meant. I like wine myself.'

'It's for a dinner. I have asked the Miltons over. It's easier for me to tell you now, it'll save you another journey.'

Jack surprised her by ignoring the comment. He stood up to leave. 'The filter coffee's better,' he said, 'but thanks anyway. And Rose?'

'Yes?'

'Don't get involved. I don't think you realise quite what you're dealing with.'

So that was the reason for this appearance; to warn her off. Did he already know something? He had not said she was not to socialise with the Miltons, therefore there was no reason not to go ahead.

When she lay in bed that night she went over all she had learnt, but it was what she had not found out that puzzled her. It might be that tomorrow evening would provide the solution.

Before she fell asleep she thought about sex. She missed it, missed David's warm body next to hers, although she had not done so during the months of his illness. Too many other things had taken priority then. Since his death she had been out with only one man – apart from Barry, with whom her relationship was platonic – and Rose knew she had been rushing things. Lonely and miserable, she had tried to find a replacement. Within a fortnight she knew that a husband could not be replaced, that one day, in the distant future, she might meet someone whom she wanted to live with or even marry, but he would not be a substitute, he would be someone she loved.

Living alone had made her selfish, made her think it would be ideal to have a man for company when she required it and who would fulfil her baser needs when necessary without making any demands on her. She smiled to herself. But I wouldn't like a man who allowed me to treat him that way, she thought.

She had no idea how sex had come into her head. And she didn't even like Jack Pearce.

Rose hummed as she worked with the radio on, enjoying the distraction of preparing three courses. Hopefully Dennis and Paul would have regained their appetites. Would they notice if she wore the same outfit she had bought for the party? Anna might, but not the men, surely, and it did not matter, as long as it did not act as a reminder.

'Come in.' Rose held open the front door, suddenly experiencing nervousness at entertaining three people she hardly knew.

'I brought some wine,' Dennis said. 'And it really is very kind of you to have us. I didn't know as many people as Gabrielle, but I get the feeling we're being avoided,' he added as she showed them into the sitting-room.

'People don't always know what to say. They feel embarrassed.'

'I expect you're right.'

'Anna, I didn't get a chance to speak to you before. I'm glad you could come.' Rose's social graces seemed to be in order. She poured drinks and explained they would be eating in the kitchen. Then she excused herself to attend to the food. Anna, she thought, was polite enough but not a great conversationalist. With her figure and colouring she was stunning but seemed a little ill at ease, although that was understandable. Satisfied that the table looked elegant and that there was nothing lying around which shouldn't have been, she told them that the meal was ready.

Dennis initiated the conversation once they were seated, commenting again on how comfortable and welcoming Rose's home was. He was more relaxed, less grey-faced than before; Paul, too, had lost some of his tenseness and was, on this third meeting, almost animated.

'Anna's had the last fitting for her dress,' he informed Rose. 'It's had to be taken in again. Pre-wedding nerves, on top of everything else, I expect.' He smiled fondly at his fiancée. 'At least she's enjoying your cooking tonight.'

'I'm not a very good cook,' Anna admitted, 'but I'm learning. If we find someone like Mrs Clarke she won't be there all the time. Still, I expect as Paul makes more and more business contacts we'll also eat out quite a lot.'

There was an uncomfortable pause which Anna misinterpreted. Father and son exchanged a quick glance but neither spoke of Paul's financial difficulties.

They had eaten a seafood salad. Rose cleared away the plates and poured more wine before dishing up roast lamb spiked with slivers of garlic and several bowls of vegetables. She had not prepared a roast for years; as Doreen Clarke had produced a plain and simple meal she had not risked anything too rich in case it was not to the Miltons' taste. Hopefully she had not overdone the garlic.

Saturday night and I'm jollying along a bereaved man, his virtually bankrupt son and his beautiful but edgy girlfriend, Rose thought as she carved the meat, not very neatly.

Handing around the plates she smiled at the irony. It was herself she had believed needed cheering up. Perhaps she should take up good works as a full-time occupation, it must be good for the soul.

'What is it you do, Paul?' Only when she had asked the question did Rose realise Gareth may have mentioned her visit. She had given a different name but DI Pearce knew about it: presumably Gareth had provided a description.

'I'm in the property business. In London.' It sounded impressive put like that.

'And you, Anna?' Rose handed her the mint sauce.

'I'm with a firm of fashion buyers. We're working on the summer collections now.'

'It must be difficult, always being several seasons ahead.'

'You get used to it.'

Rose wondered how the pastel outfit stood up to inspection. Anna was wearing a coat-dress. 'So, has anything been decided about the house yet?' No mention had been made of the photographs she had taken. Rose would have to cut her losses.

'I'll have to sell,' replied Dennis. 'I've been on to my office. Well, to be frank, I took the bull by the horns and asked if the rumours were true. I explained I needed to know my position. It'll be put in writing, but I shall, as they phrased it, be taking voluntary redundancy. With that, and what I make from the sale of both properties, I'll get a small place down here and take my chances. I wouldn't be happy in London now.'

'But Gabrielle said—'

Dennis interrupted whatever Anna had been about to say. 'Whatever Gabrielle said doesn't count. She has left everything to me.'

'No!' Anna thumped the table. 'No. That's impossible.'

Rose stared from one to another, her hand reaching out to steady her wineglass.

'Anna.' Dennis and Paul spoke together. Her face was scarlet.

'It's true,' Dennis said quietly. 'The police needed to know what was in the will.' There was no need to elucidate; they all knew the reasons for that. 'Maybe she intended changing it and was killed before she could do so, but I think not.'

The pallor had returned to Paul's face. 'Hasn't she left me anything at all?'

'I'm afraid not. You see, your mother and I felt we had bailed you out enough times, that you'd never be a success if we continued to do so. I think she did it for your own good.'

'It's all right, Paul.' Anna laid a hand on his arm. 'Your father won't let you down.'

'Let him down? What do you mean?' Dennis was puzzled.

Rose watched the interplay silently. It was hard to believe that she was in her own kitchen, harder still to accept that her guests were so freely discussing Gabrielle's will in front of her. Curiosity was one thing but she felt embarrassed although she did not interrupt.

'Paul needs an injection of cash if he is to succeed. Gabrielle always promised she would do the best for Paul. I'm sure you won't go back on her word, Dennis. She told me we had nothing to worry about. It won't be easy getting married if we haven't any money.'

'Other people manage.' Rose was surprised to hear her own indignant voice. 'David and I started from nothing.'

'But I expect you were used to not having very much.'

It was true but Rose still felt it was no justification for Anna to try to manipulate her future father-in-law. At least by the way the couple were looking at each other they seemed to be in love.

Paul stepped in. He could not bear to see Anna

distressed and he felt he owed an explanation for what seemed to be a mercenary streak. 'Anna's not had an easy life, I wanted to repair that damage. She found out accidentally that she was adopted but her sister wasn't. Her parents claimed they wanted to wait until she was older to tell her. You can imagine the shock.'

Rose could, but others survived unscarred, and money would not heal that particular trauma.

'After that she lived with an aunt and then, just when she thought she'd finally found security, the person she was going to marry let her down. You can see why money has become important.'

I can understand, Rose thought, but she's also using the past to gain sympathy. She wondered if Anna realised the pain she must have caused her adoptive parents who had cared for her and loved her. But she would not judge too harshly even though Anna seemed to show little grief or sorrow for the dead woman's family. It was obvious that she loved Paul.

Their plates were not quite empty but the food had gone cold so Rose removed them from the table; she regretted issuing the invitation. Turning back from the draining board she saw the faces of all three before they had a chance to compose themselves. Dennis was staring at the young couple with a mixture of bewilderment and despair; Anna was tight-lipped, upright in her chair, while Paul reached out and took her hand. There were two spots of colour across his high cheekbones yet he did not seem angry.

'Would anyone like coffee?' Rose wanted them to leave and decided not to offer them the fruit salad she had made.

'No, I think we ought to go.' Dennis stood. 'It was a lovely meal, Rose. Thank you. I'm sorry if we appeared rude.'

At the front door Paul shook her hand and thanked her too but was obviously anxious to get Anna on her own. Anna smiled weakly and waited for the men to walk on to the car. Then she turned to face Rose. 'I enjoyed the meal and I appreciate your concern for the family but I don't think you're being very fair to Dennis.'

'Oh?' Rose blinked in surprise.

'It's too soon after Gabrielle's death to expect him to be interested in other women.' Before Rose could answer Anna had hurried down the path.

Rose stood motionless in the doorway. Was that how Anna saw her? As a single woman who was only interested in Dennis for his money, perhaps hoping to marry him for that reason? She shook her head in disbelief. It had been a disastrous evening and one she did not intend to repeat. Besides, Anna seemed unaware of Dennis's own financial position. Unless he managed to find another job locally he would have to invest whatever he inherited wisely. Then another thought occurred to her: just how much did Gabrielle have to leave? There might be a considerable sum as well as the house.

'Don't,' she said aloud as she scraped the food from the plates into the bin. 'Don't think about it.'

She could not face the washing up. Once the remains of the joint were in the fridge and the fruit salad dish covered with film she went to the sitting-room and sat in the dark looking out over the soothing aspect of the harbour and the bay until some sort of peace returned.

CHAPTER EIGHT

'I'm going to bed,' Anna said as soon as they reached the house.

'I need to talk to you.'

'Not now, Paul. In the morning.'

Paul went to join his father in the lounge but there was nothing to be gained there either. Dennis sat staring moodily towards the drawn curtains unable to cope with the conflicting emotions he was experiencing. For the first time the real magnitude of what had happened hit him and he realised he would never see Gabrielle again. Maggie no longer counted, she would not be part of his future. She must have guessed that by now but when Paul had gone to bed he would telephone her to make it clear. It was only fair. Strange, he thought, now it was too late, he wanted to do the right thing by everyone.

'The police don't seem to be doing very much, do

they?' Paul wanted to get his father talking. He had tried, on the night his mother was killed, to ask him for a loan or for payment in advance of whatever money he was due to inherit later. But he did not want to dive straight in with a request for cash.

'They wouldn't tell us if they were. We're all suspects. Why do you think they keep coming back? Look, Paul, I'm not in the mood for conversation, on this or any other topic. If you don't mind, I'd like to be alone.'

Paul shrugged and left the room. Tomorrow would have to do, although he had hoped to be able to tell Anna everything was sorted out.

Dennis poured a brandy, knowing he did not need or want it. What he did need was a night's sleep but the bedroom he was using felt wrong. At first he had been forbidden use of his own room but now the police tape had been removed he could not face the double bed he had shared with Gabrielle. Sometimes he stood in the doorway and, although he was sure it was not possible, he thought her perfume lingered in the air. What he did know was that all pretence of being a happy family had gone.

Rose woke to a clear blue sky and a boisterous wind. She opened several windows, thinking that a through-draught would rid the house of the contamination of last night's visitors.

Studying her face in the bathroom mirror she thought she looked tired, but otherwise the same Rose. She had never been beautiful, but she had grown into her looks and men considered her to be attractive. She had always been comfortable with her body and face and had not really given them much thought. She groaned as she remembered the dishes waiting to be washed. And there was a baby to be photographed. Sunday was the only time that was convenient for the family, which Rose found odd. However, work was work.

Dishes done, she threw on an old jacket and drove into Penzance. That was the only problem with the photography side: the equipment was too heavy to lug about on foot.

The baby was plump and dimpled. 'She's born to it,' Rose told the mother as the child gazed straight at her, gurgling and beaming. It was to be a record of her first birthday.

The wind was dying down and there were quite a few people enjoying a walk along the front. Further out were several white-sailed yachts. She promised herself a long walk after lunch, a lunch which would consist of cold lamb and salad.

She had been tempted to have a quiet word with Dennis, to let him know Gabrielle had sent the invitation to Maggie Anderson, but that would be playing into Maggie's hands. And it might not be true. Rose had guessed Maggie wanted her to put in a good word for her. And Gabrielle was no longer around to defend herself.

Rose braked suddenly. She had almost crossed the roundabout without giving way to an oncoming car.

What if Dennis knew that his wife knew about Maggie? What if Dennis also knew that his wife was about to change her will in Paul's favour for that very reason? How much more of a motive did that give him, especially as he was concerned about losing his job?

Stop being melodramatic, she told herself. The police had to be aware of these facts. Yet they had not arrested Dennis. She reminded herself that there were about forty people present that evening, apart from anyone who might have arrived unseen.

She seemed to recall that the inquest was to be held soon. How long would it be before Gabrielle was allowed a funeral? Rose was not sure if she would attend: they were not close, but it might be rude not to. It would be the first since David's.

She should have known that she would pass Laura, who was on her way up to see her. Trevor had been home for several days but was now back at sea.

'You've been out early for a Sunday,' Laura said as she climbed into the passenger seat.

'I had a job.'

'How did it go? With the Milton clan?'

'Don't even talk about it.'

'That bad?'

'That bad. How's things with you?'

'Improving. I tarted myself up and persuaded Trevor to take me out for a meal. We've had a long talk and we've both agreed to make some compromises. It's not exactly bliss, but it's one hell of a lot better than it has been.'

'Good.'

Laura looked at her slyly. 'Jack Pearce was asking about you.'

'I heard.' They had reached the house. Rose pulled on the handbrake and killed the ignition. She turned to meet Laura's eyes. 'And what exactly did you tell him?'

'Only what he wanted to hear. That you aren't a murderess. Like I said, he fancies you. Now come on, woman, I'm gasping for a cup of coffee.'

There were no messages on the answering machine, for which Rose was grateful. An hour with Laura, then she would have the afternoon to herself. If it didn't rain she would clear the tubs of the summer flowers which were becoming brown and untidy.

Laura sensed her friend was not in a communicative mood. 'You're not upset, are you?'

'About what?'

'About me discussing you with Jack. I didn't say anything that you couldn't have listened to.'

'No, I'm not upset.' She smiled to show it was true.

Laura got up to leave. Rose watched her bob down the path, her long legs thin in her leggings, her hair blowing this way and that in the blustery wind. She looks better, Rose thought, happier. She wondered just how serious her problems had been.

She was staring into the fridge when a tap on the side window made her jump. 'Oh, sodding hell,' she said, hoping it was loud enough for Jack Pearce to have heard her. 'Yes? What is it now?'

'May I come in?'

Rose did not answer. He took this to mean yes. 'I'm not staying. I was on my way to my mother's actually. Mr Milton asked me to give you this.' He handed her an envelope. Rose took it from him, frowning in confusion. It was unaddressed. She tore it open with her thumbnail. Inside was a cheque, made out to her and for a sum which meant nothing.

'He said it was for the photographs.'

'But he's only had the proofs.'

Jack shrugged. 'Nothing to do with me. He simply said he remembered you hadn't been paid for your work and apologised for leaving it so long.'

'He could have posted it, or brought it personally.'

'He wasn't sure if that was possible.'

'Why? What's happened? Where is Dennis?'

'He's in Camborne at the moment.' He waited to see what her reaction would be.

Rose realised the implications of what he was saying. Dennis, then, was helping with inquiries or whatever euphemism it was they used for hauling someone in. His remembering she had not been paid could be interpreted in converse ways: a guilty man wishing to repay any debts before being locked up, an innocent man remembering a chore because he had nothing else on his conscience. She was not going to ask.

'In case you believe we're not doing anything, we're going through a process of elimination.'

'Like Sherlock Holmes, no doubt.'

'I'm sorry?'

'You know, when you've ruled out the impossible, whatever remains, however improbable, must be the answer. Something like that, I can't remember.'

'Are you a Conan Doyle fan?'

'Not particularly. And I don't wish to spend Sunday afternoon discussing literature. Besides, your mother'll have your dinner on the table by now.'

Jack Pearce's mouth tightened. He exhaled slowly, then said, 'I do not expect my mother to run around after me. I'm taking her out to lunch. Then I shall spend the afternoon playing cards with her. She's almost eighty and half crippled with arthritis and she's lost most of her friends. I suspect she's lonely and I am unable to see her as often as I'd like.'

'I'm sorry.' Rose turned away. What a bitch I am, she thought, and a hypocrite. She had shown no mercy to Anna either.

'It's OK, you weren't to know.' And then he spoilt it. 'I did use to have a wife to run around after me, though.'

When Rose looked up she saw he was smiling and changed her mind about the retort she had been about to make. And now he had made his marital status clear to her. Why? 'Used to?'

'She left me.' There were no excuses, no explanations, just the honest statement.

'I'm widowed.'

'Yes, I know.'

Of course he did, he would have made inquiries into

the background of everyone who was at the party. 'Well, you'd better not keep your mother waiting.'

'Hint taken. I don't know why you're so prickly with me, Rose. I find it strange when everyone tells me what a nice person you are.'

She did not rise to the bait. No way was she going to ask who else he had been discussing her with. 'Inspector Pearce, I hope you're not going to formally arrest Dennis Milton. He didn't do it, you know.'

'Oh?'

'I'm sure he didn't.'

'Ah, the old gut reaction. Still, it's often right. Now, I really must go.' He managed to make it sound as if she had deliberately been trying to detain him. 'You'll be pleased to know we no longer consider you to be a suspect.'

'I—'

'But you are still a witness. However, I'd like to take you out to dinner, as a friend. And if anyone asks, I'm making further inquiries. May I telephone you tomorrow for your answer?'

'I—' For the second time Rose was lost for words. The door crashed behind him before she could speak.

Later that afternoon she telephoned the Milton house. Doreen Clarke answered. 'No one's here at the minute. Can I take a message?'

'No, it's all right, thanks, Doreen, I'll call back later.'

'Have you heard?'

160

'Heard what?' She might have to explain from whom she had heard if she admitted anything.

'All hell's broken loose over this way. First Mr Milton gets taken away in a police car, then Eileen Penrose's shot her mouth off and got Jim dragged into it too. Well, there's nothing in it, of course, we all know why she's done it.' Rose had lost track of the conversation but knew Doreen would continue anyway. 'Eileen found out Jim had taken another woman out. She must've told the police he was always at it and coupled his name with Mrs Milton's. Me and Cyril think she's probably gone and told them he was up at the house that night. He *was* out with someone though, me and a friend saw him.'

'I expect the police'll sort it out. 'Bye now.' Could it be that simple? Rose wondered when she replaced the receiver. Was this Jim Penrose a womaniser, one with a jealous wife, one who needed to kill his lover to prevent her from dropping him in it? For now Rose had other things on her mind. What answer was she going to give Jack Pearce tomorrow?

Jim Penrose had walked brazenly and deliberately into the pub knowing that at that time of night there would be quite a few customers he knew. He had met Rita Chynoweth by chance in another pub. Although there was no proof that she shared her sexual favours with anyone who asked, rumour declared it was so. Rita was unperturbed and had taken to dressing the part: tight jeans over amply fleshed thighs were complemented by a white knitted top which stopped short of her midriff, exposing a comfortable roll of brown flesh which rested on a studded leather belt. Around her shoulders was a red leather jacket. On her arm was Jim Penrose.

Seeing Doreen and Teresa in the corner had prompted her to clutch at her escort as they came through the door. She flung back her hair, which was dyed a reddish purple.

Jim had noticed the women too. It would be interesting to see what Eileen had to say when presented with what she would assume was unquestionable proof of his guilt.

It took several days before it got back to Eileen when she overheard, as she was meant to, a conversation in the greengrocer's. She purchased her vegetables and went home planning Jim's punishment.

When he came in for his evening meal he saw by her face that things were not right but, surprisingly, she said nothing. An hour later the police arrived.

Rose telephoned the author she had photographed and asked if it was convenient for her to bring around the contact sheet from which he could make his choice. It was ready but there was no hurry, Rose simply wanted to be out of the house in case Jack rang early. She had not made up her mind what to say to him.

She was out no more than an hour. The light on the answering machine glowed but was not flashing. No one had telephoned.

It was not until six fifteen whilst she was clearing up

watercolours and brushes from the table where she had been completing some sketches that the telephone rang.

'Hello?'

'Rose? It's me, Jack.'

She waited.

'Are you free this evening?'

'This evening?' She hadn't washed her hair. Which means, she thought, that I intended saying yes.

'I know it's short notice, but I can't guarantee another night this week.'

'I . . . er . . . OK.'

'Good. I'll pick you up about eight. Anywhere you particularly like?'

'No.'

She ran a bath and looked through the small cupboard in her bedroom which served as a wardrobe. She picked a skirt, gathered at the waist, in striking shades of orange and red and black. It wasn't really the weather for boots but she had no suitable shoes to go with it. Her top was a black leotard.

She was ready by seven thirty and tried to read but found herself watching the minutes ticking by on the carriage clock on the mantelpiece.

Jack Pearce was fifteen minutes late.

'I'm sorry. Work.'

'It's all right.' Rose was cool; she was not sure whether she would have preferred him not to have turned up. It was all too unsettling.

'Can we call a truce?' Jack asked as they headed

towards Penzance. 'And I would appreciate your opinion on some of the people involved.'

'I see. You want me to be your . . . what's the word? Grass? Informer?'

Jack laughed loudly. 'You slay me, Rose Trevelyan. I just meant that, being an artist, you must have an eye for detail.'

'Oh.'

'I bought my wife one of your paintings once.'

'You did? Which one was it?' Rose, like many artists, had her work on display in local shops and cafes. Occasionally she sold a few that way, others were commissioned through word of mouth or sold via galleries which handled several artists' work.

'I don't know. It was a view of Land's End. Before it was ruined,' he added, referring to the theme park.

'You feel the same as me, then. I suppose tourists need things like that but I liked it as it was. Just the cliffs and the sea.'

'And the signpost.'

'Oh, yes, and the signpost.' Under which visitors could stand and have a picture taken. Inserted would be the name of their home town and the distance away in miles. Rose realised it was the first time they had had any sort of interaction which did not involve the Miltons in some way and was not tense with undercurrents.

'Marian – that's my wife, ex-wife – she said, now don't take offence, she said it was a little on the crude side but that's what appealed to her. She said it showed feeling and you probably enjoyed painting it. I don't know anything about art myself, but I liked it too.'

'Thank you.' Was the flattery genuine? 'It was done a long time ago, not long after I came down here. I love wild landscapes. Unfortunately I can only make a real living out of photography.'

'Will a curry suit you?' Jack had slowed the car. He needed to know where to park.

'Yes, fine.'

'A drink first, though – I can't imagine you refusing.'

She glanced at his face – lined, pleasant – but could not see his eyes as he turned to reverse into a space on the sea front.

They walked up the hill, several feet apart, Rose wishing she had brought a jacket. The evenings were cooler now and the heat of the previous weeks seemed to have become a thing of the past.

'Barry Rowe told me you do a good line in greetings cards too. That you paint them and he reproduces them.'

'Did he now?'

'He's very fond of you.'

'And I of him. I've known him for over twenty years.'

'Your boyfriend?'

'Boyfriend? At my age? No, just a good friend.'

They entered the Union Hotel and Jack went to the bar leaving Rose to pick a table.

'Is there one?' he asked when he returned with a pint

of bitter and a glass of red wine. 'A boyfriend?'

'Not at the moment.' Let him make of that what he liked, she thought as she sipped the red wine she had not asked for. He was taking a lot on to assume he knew her tastes.

There was silence for several minutes. Jack was taller than her with dark springy hair, plenty of it for his age, she considered, guessing that he might be older than herself but that there were not many years between them.

'Me neither,' he volunteered. 'I've been divorced for twelve years, I don't seem to have the time for women somehow.'

Was this another veiled compliment?

'Anyway, as I said, what do you make of the Miltons?'

Not a compliment, Rose realised. She was here to give him information, information he supposed she possessed but was keeping to herself. 'I feel sorry for Dennis. He regrets his affair.'

'No doubt he does. Now.'

'I think he was manipulated into it. Maggie gives the impression she knows how to handle people. Paul? Well, to be honest, I think he's just a fool.'

Jack smiled as she took another sip of wine. So far, their opinions coincided. Enough of work, that was not the real reason he had invited her out. 'How long have you lived here?'

'Since I left college. I've never imagined being able to leave.'

'I didn't realise how much I loved it, either, not until

I moved away. Come on, I'll tell you about it while we eat.'

They walked on to the Indian restaurant, where they ordered a main course each and opted to share a portion of rice and a couple of vegetables. 'Why did you leave?' Rose asked.

'Usual story. I was young, thought life was lived elsewhere and that there was nothing here worth staying for. I went to London, then north. Leeds. I was in the force by then and that's where I met my wife. We got married, had a couple of kids and then, sounds daft, but I was homesick. I requested a transfer and finally got it. Marian wasn't keen, she's a city girl, but she was prepared to give it a try. I pointed out the benefits of bringing the children up down here. Well, it all went wrong. I'm not blaming her. I think she felt the same way about her home as I did mine. Anyway, we decided to call it a day.'

'And your children?'

'The boys? They were fourteen and thirteen when Marian left. They took it better than we'd imagined. They'd spent most of their lives in Leeds so it wasn't an entirely new start for them.'

'Do you see them?' Rose hoped she wasn't asking questions which might cause pain.

'Oh, yes. They used to come for holidays, begrudgingly at first. My mother looked after them if I was working, then they got involved in water sports and surfing and, of course, in the summer, there were girls. Funny to think

167

they're men now. Twenty-five and twenty-six. Makes me feel ancient.'

'So you're about fifty?'

'Exactly. Had the big birthday last month.'

'Equals us up a bit.'

'What?'

'You got all my personal details from that first interview.'

A waiter placed hot-plates on the table, then brought the food. Jack watched. Yes, he was right. Rose, having been told they were very hot, was one of those people who just had to touch. She drew her finger back quickly and placed her hands in her lap. 'I know it's daft,' she said, aware he had seen her, 'but you're no different.'

'How come?' He leant forward, elbows on the table.

'When you sat down you automatically pushed your knife and fork in a bit. You watch, loads of people do that.'

'*Touché*. Like I said, you're a very observant lady.'

'I was trained to be.'

'So was I.'

Stalemate, Rose thought as she helped herself to prawn dopiaza.

Jack Pearce ran her home, watched her safely to the door and departed without getting out of the car. Rose Trevelyan, he thought, as he made his way back to his flat, knows more than she is saying. What made him so sure was not what she had told him, but what she had not mentioned. And how come, if she was on friendly terms with the Miltons, she had not asked whether Dennis was still being held?

CHAPTER NINE

Rose's mood the following morning was carefree and she knew she was now not going to fall into the pit which threatened each year. The anniversary was behind her. She had wanted to ask Jack what was going to happen to Dennis but did not wish to spoil the evening by referring back to that subject.

She wrote a receipt for the cheque she had received, although it was not necessary, and used it as an excuse to visit the Milton household. Anna's rudeness still rankled; it would be interesting to meet her on her own ground. But she was genuinely concerned about Dennis.

Ignoring Jack Pearce's warning to keep out of things, she drove to Gwithian and pulled into the driveway. The mobile police unit was no longer there, which made her think an arrest might have taken place.

'Mrs Trevelyan.' Doreen Clarke dried her hands on an apron. 'Mr Milton's out. I don't know what to do.' Her round face was creased with worry. 'Come in. Come out to the kitchen for a minute. No one'll disturb us there. Least of all madam.'

The kitchen had every appliance a cook could wish for. Rose was impressed.

'I expect you'd like some coffee.' Doreen obviously wanted to detain her. 'I don't know whether to go in there or not.' She nodded vaguely towards the hall. 'The two of them were shouting at each other.'

'Who?'

'Anna, and the other one. Maggie something or other.'

'Maggie?'

'Turned up demanding to see Dennis. She said she had something she wanted to tell him. Anna asked her to leave, she said whatever it was could be done over the phone. She refused to go, said it wasn't Anna's house. That's when the shouting started.'

Rose wasn't surprised. If Anna had been expecting the house to be left to Paul she would wonder how Maggie knew otherwise. 'Where are they now?'

'I don't know. I heard footsteps on the stairs. I suppose Anna's gone to her room. Can you do anything?'

'Me? Like what?'

Doreen held out her hands in a gesture of helplessness. 'I don't know. Talk to them? I don't want poor Mr Milton to walk back into this. They let him go, you know. I don't know how they could've thought he'd done it. Maggie or no Maggie,' she added firmly.

So Doreen, too, was aware of the affair. 'Where's Paul?'

'He's gone into Redruth for something. He didn't say when he'd be back.'

Just as Doreen handed her a cup of coffee the kitchen door opened.

'Good heavens. What's going on? There seems little chance of much privacy in this house.'

'I didn't mean to intrude,' Rose replied.

'That's what the other one said.'

Rose placed her cup and saucer gently on the table. 'I'm not sure why you don't like me, Anna, but it wasn't you I came to see.'

'No. Dennis again, of course. I'd prefer it if you left.'

'You're right, it is Dennis and it's up to him to decide whether or not he wishes to see me. He needs friends at the moment, not histrionics from young girls.'

Doreen gasped, half in shock, half in pleasure. Good for Mrs Trevelyan, she thought.

'I'm sorry,' Anna managed to say. 'It isn't easy at the moment.'

'It isn't easy for anyone, knowing that there is still a murderer out there. Their grievance may not rest with Gabrielle alone.'

'Oh, really? And how come you're such a damn expert?'

'I do not claim to be an expert, I'm simply here to offer

Dennis assistance because it's obviously not forthcoming from his future daughter-in-law.'

'Get out.' Anna hissed the words.

Rose hesitated, then, feeling Doreen's hand touch her arm briefly, stood her ground. 'I'm staying until Mr Milton returns.' The door slammed behind Anna, and Rose and Doreen exchanged a look of relief mingled with uncertainty. 'See what I mean?' Doreen said. 'I don't know what to do, who to let in or anything. Mr Milton left me no instructions.'

'And he's going to return to find two uninvited women in his house. Doreen, would it be all right if I went through to the lounge? I might as well chat to Maggie.'

'Of course, Mrs Trevelyan.'

'Oh, call me Rose, it's too much of a mouthful.'

Doreen was pleased. She would be able to tell her friends she was on first-name terms with a real artist.

'Maggie?' Rose had opened the door quietly. The woman was seated on the edge of a settee, head bowed. 'Sorry, I didn't mean to startle you.'

'What a mess it all is. It's crazy, I can't keep away from the place. Despite that girl. At least they've let Dennis go but from what I've heard, it might not be for long. And it's all my fault. The police suspected me and all I've done is to make them think it's Dennis.'

'How was that?' Rose joined her on the settee.

'Other guests have confirmed that at one point we were both missing from the room. It's true, and I told the police. I followed him because I wanted to put him straight, to let him know Gabrielle knew. The looks he was giving me! I thought if she did know and hadn't made any fuss, she might be willing to let him go.'

'That's not what you told me, Maggie. You said Gabrielle had invited you to put you at a disadvantage, to let Dennis see what he'd be losing if he went off with you.'

'I know. And that's true. I'm sure that's why she did it, but what I just said holds true as well.'

'You really did receive an invitation?'

'Yes.' She looked surprised.

'You haven't exactly stuck to the truth, you see.'

'No. I was only trying to protect everyone, including myself.' She reached for her handbag which was on the floor beside her. 'Here.' She handed Rose the deckle-edged card, still in its envelope.

Rose had not seen one; her invitation had come via the telephone. The printing was done in black sloping letters, only the name of the recipient had been filled in by hand. The address on the envelope was typed. 'Did you show this to the police?'

'Yes. Once they knew about me and Dennis, and Dennis denied he'd asked me, I had to. They thought I'd gate-crashed.'

It wasn't Dennis's writing. Even though there were only three words from which to judge they were not written by the same person who had written out the cheque she had received. Dennis wrote in large, sprawled characters and there was hardly enough room for him to sign his name on the bottom.

'You said Paul knew. About you and Dennis.'

'If he didn't know, he must have guessed. He saw us together. We were in a restaurant. Unfortunately we were holding hands at the time. God, you don't think Paul sent it? Why would he do that?'

'I don't know. To show his father what he was doing was wrong, maybe?' But Rose did not think so. She had other ideas. 'There's a car. That must be Dennis.'

'Stay with me, will you, while I talk to him?'

'I don't think that would—'

'Please, Rose.'

Maggie had become agitated and the appeal in her eyes could not be ignored.

'All right.'

They heard voices in the hall, one male, one female. Doreen Clarke must also have heard the car and warned her employer.

'Hello.' Dennis came into the room. His face was expressionless and he looked exhausted.

'Maggie has something to say to you. She asked if I'd stay while she did so.' Rose then clasped her hands together and closed her mouth. She had done her bit.

'Dennis, I appreciate your telephone call the other night. I understand how you feel.'

'Do you? I doubt that. Your wife hasn't been killed.'

'No. I meant about me. I just wanted . . . Jesus, this

isn't easy. I just wanted to say that I never meant to hurt anyone. I didn't give Gabrielle a thought when it started. I'm sorry. And I'm sorry if I said anything to the police which misled them. I couldn't telephone, I wanted to say it to your face. Besides, I thought you'd hang up. I accept it's over, Dennis, and I won't trouble you again.'

'You came all the way down here just to tell me that?'

'Yes. I didn't want it to end the way it had.'

Rose was as surprised as Dennis appeared to be. She had imagined Maggie was going to come out with something a little more earth-shattering. However, it had probably salved her conscience a little.

'And in the process I've upset Anna.' But Maggie did not offer an apology on that count. 'I'll go now.'

Dennis nodded and held the door open for her. From where she was sitting Rose saw Maggie look back once. She thought she might have been crying.

'Rose?'

'I just happened to be here. I came to see if there was anything I could do to help. I didn't know if they'd kept you at Camborne.'

'No. But they've asked me to remain here. It doesn't matter. Paul's not back yet?'

'No. Dennis, Anna asked me to leave, but I said I'd prefer to wait and see you. I hope I haven't added to your problems.'

'Anna has no right to do that. Ignore her. She's neurotic at times and I think she's very frightened.

Despite what Paul told you the other night, she's led a sheltered life. This has upset her, and she's getting in a state about the wedding.'

'It's still on?'

Dennis glanced at her sharply. 'Yes. Of course. Thank you, Rose.'

'For what?'

'For coming. For taking an interest. I'm very much in need of a friend right now. Paul's got Anna to consider and my colleagues in London don't seem to be returning my calls.'

No, Rose thought. She had seen it before. People felt threatened in such situations. Dennis's wife had been murdered, he himself was being considered as a suspect, and he was about to be made redundant. He was probably regarded as a loser and no one wanted that sort of luck to rub off on them. How lucky she had been in her own friends when David died. 'You've got my number. I'd better go now.' She had forgotten the pretext of the receipt in her bag.

There was so much to think about. Ought she to tell Jack what she suspected? No, he would be annoyed. Jack. Already she had dropped the Inspector Pearce bit. And tonight she was repaying Barry for the meal he had cooked and the two he had insisted on buying in London. On the second evening he had outwitted her by asking for the bill on the way out to the toilet and paying it upon his return.

* * *

Barry arrived promptly at seven thirty and she poured him a can of beer she had got in especially. 'Go and sit down while I finish out here,' she told him. It was dusk; the table lamps were already on and the artificial coals of the gas fire glowed, although there was no need for the fire itself.

Ten minutes later Rose joined him. 'I went to see Dennis today.'

'How nice.'

'He doesn't have anyone else to turn to.'

'He's got a son, and the girlfriend, and a housekeeper. Three more than I've got.'

'Whatever's the matter with you?'

'You might've told me.'

'Told you what?'

'Not only are you hob-nobbing with the Miltons, which doesn't look too good so soon after Gabrielle's death, but you're going out with the bloke who's running the case.'

'I see.' Rose stared at her drink. Wherever she turned lately people started having a go at her. 'My social life is my own affair, Barry. I don't have to answer to you. And I am not going out with Jack Pearce, as you put it. He took me for a meal because he wanted to discuss a few things.'

'I bet he did.'

'If you're going to be like this all evening I can't see there's much point in your staying.'

'Sorry, Rosie. I just hate it when you get obsessed about

things. I feel I'm losing you. I value your friendship, you see, more than you may realise.'

She understood but said nothing. This was not just about friendship; Barry was jealous. Seeing his familiar face, the hair brushed over his scalp, the glasses already slipping, she wondered if a different kind of relationship was possible. He was attentive and kind and understanding and punctual. Not once in either business or pleasure had he let her down. But look how he was tonight, and how he had been on other occasions. If they were together permanently she suspected he would want to know where she was every minute of the day. No can do, she thought, as a picture of Jack Pearce's face came into her mind.

'And I'm worried about you, Rose.'

'Worried?'

'When you get your teeth into something, you won't let go. It's unhealthy. And', he added, sitting upright as if the thought had just occurred to him, 'you could be in danger.'

Rose frowned. She had told Anna that the murderer had not yet been caught. Barry might be right. And was that why Jack had warned her off? But what did anyone have to fear from her?

'OK. We won't talk about it any more. Have you had any comeback from the trade fair yet?'

'A couple of orders have trickled in. It takes a while. Don't forget, I picked up several while we were there.'

She had forgotten. She had been too busy thinking

about other things. 'How did you know about Jack?' That subject could not be dropped until her curiosity had been satisfied.

'You were seen.'

Rose laughed. 'You make it sound so ominous. *You were seen.*' She mimicked his tone. 'I wasn't doing anything people can't know about.'

'They'll know all right.'

'Right. The food's almost ready. If you're going to sulk you can go, if not you can join me. Now act your age and drink that beer. There's three more cans in the kitchen.'

He smiled sheepishly. 'What've we got?'

'Bacon, with apple and red cabbage. It's Polish, I think.'

'And the wine?'

'The Co-op's finest. But plentiful.' Rose sighed. The status quo had been restored.

An hour later it was completely dark and there was a stillness outside. The window was open because the kitchen was over-warm from the oven being on. They both looked up when they heard the first drops of rain hit the glass. They were followed by a clap of thunder which made Rose jump. Lightning illuminated the garden for a split second. The storm had started almost immediately overhead. Sometimes they would last for hours, just rolling round the bay, not affecting other areas. The lights flickered. Rose got up and fetched a couple of night-lights from the drawer, along with a box of matches. They were safer than candles and had originally come with a food warmer she never used. She would not be badly affected if the electricity did go off; both cooker and heating were gas and the water in the immersion heater would stay hot until at least the morning.

They went through to the sitting-room and stood in the window, watching the violence which was taking place outside. The lights flickered again and went out. At one point Rose thought Barry was about to speak. He touched her shoulder, then changed his mind. She was glad. If he made any sort of romantic declaration their relationship would change.

'Come on, there's still some more beer. I'll finish the wine.'

'You've had most of the bottle.'

'Oh, don't you start! Jack . . .' but she, too, did not complete what she had been about to say. She had bitten her tongue too late.

'Are you seeing him again?' Barry asked quietly.

Only then did it occur to Rose that no mention of a further meeting had taken place. 'I don't think so.' She hid her dismay by pouring out the last of the wine. 'He might need to ask a few more questions, I suppose.'

It was an appropriate time for power to be restored. It would probably go again. The fluorescent tube buzzed and lit itself with a twang. The flames from the night-lights seemed paltry by comparison. She blew them out, liking the acrid tang of the wisps of smoke from the burnt wicks.

'See you over the weekend?' Barry asked as he left.

'Not Saturday. I'm going out with Laura.'

He shook his head but refrained from commenting, other than to say goodnight.

Rose had said to Barry that the rain was too heavy to last. Her prediction was correct. Puddles lay on the lawn and in the pot-holes of her drive but they reflected a watery sun. She needed some fresh air, to get away and paint in solitude. First she did some overdue housework. Surfaces dusted, carpets vacuumed and the bathroom gleaming, she pinned her hair up, put on a waterproof jacket and loaded what she needed into the back of the Mini. It refused to start.

'Bugger it.' Rose got out and sprayed the relevant parts of the engine with Damp-Start. When she turned the ignition it whined but refused to kick into life.

Back inside she rang Laura's number. There wasn't an engine that baffled Trevor, on land or at sea.

'Of course he will,' Laura said. 'But he won't be back for two more days. Can you manage? If you need a lift I'll take you.'

'No. I'll cope.' It was a nuisance, but she'd walk somewhere. Trevor would sort it out when he came home. She tried the ignition once more on her way out but it sounded worse, just a slow whirr, then nothing.

It took about half an hour to walk to Abbey Basin. Rose had decided to get a bus somewhere. The harbour was to her right. She changed her mind: she would sketch that, then have a coffee somewhere in the town. Would Jack be like Barry? she thought, as she began to work. Surely not. With his irregular hours he could not expect anyone else to be at his beck and call. It was hypothetical anyway, he was not going to ring her again.

When she returned she found there had been three calls in her absence. Two were jobs, the third was from Jack. 'You're busy, I'll catch you some other time,' was all he said after he'd given his name.

Jim Penrose had been allowed to go home but only after he had spent several hours being questioned. Eileen may have thought she was paying him back but she had only made herself look a fool. On the night of Gabrielle's party, knowing his wife would be working at the house, he had arranged to do a job for a friend in St Erth. He had run into difficulties and it had taken an hour longer than he had estimated. Afterwards, as thanks for his efforts, his friend had bought him a drink. It would be checked, but Jim Penrose could not have been at the Milton place that evening if what he claimed was true.

'Well?' Eileen sniffed when he returned. 'I'm surprised they didn't lock you up.' She moved across to the cooker and stirred something in a pan.

'Don't bother cooking on my account. Has anyone ever told you what a bitch you are?'

Eileen turned to face him, an expression of shock on her face. He was leaning against the fridge, his eyes hard.

'All those years, Eileen, and I've never laid a finger on another woman.'

'What about Rita? You can't deny that.'

'I bought Rita a few drinks. No more than that. Whether you believe me is up to you. I'm sick of making excuses for innocent things. In fact, I'm sick of you. I'm leaving you, Eileen. Oh, don't worry.' He raised a hand to stop any protests or recriminations. 'I'll make sure you don't suffer financially.'

'You can't leave me, Jim,' she whispered as he walked towards the stairs.

'I can't stay. Not with a woman who'd do that, who'd try and get the police to believe I'd killed someone.'

'I only meant—'

'It doesn't matter what you meant, you did it. I'll never forgive you for that.'

Eileen did not move. Above her head she heard his heavy tread on the worn carpet, the opening and closing of drawers and cupboards and, finally, the flushing of the toilet cistern. She loved him in her own way. The problem had been that she was never able to understand what he had seen in her. She had never been pretty and Jim was so handsome. She wasn't even really sure if she had suspected him of seeing other women.

But for once in her life Eileen Penrose could not think of a single thing to do or say to defuse the situation.

The front door closed quietly. Jim had left without even saying goodbye.

'I've changed my mind, Paul, I think we should wait. What'll people think if we get married so soon? I mean, your mother isn't buried yet.'

'You've never cared what people think, Anna. I love you, that's the only thing that matters. Don't you know I can see how all this has affected you? The sooner you're my wife, the better.'

'But, the thing is . . .' She paused. Her shiny black hair fell forward, covering her face.

'What?'

'Nothing, Paul. It doesn't matter. Look, I think I'd like to return to London.'

'Please, not yet. Just stay until the weekend. They're not expecting you back at work yet.'

Anna contemplated her fingernails. It might be better to remain. She had told the police she would be staying and the idea of being alone in her flat was not so appealing now she thought about it. 'All right.' She made an effort to smile. 'Until the weekend.'

'They'll probably have arrested someone by then. They're still going around asking a lot of questions.'

'Paul, what if they don't find who did it?'

'Of course they will.'

'Supposing it was a stranger, someone who just came by chance?'

'By chance? With a houseful of people?' But as he thought about it, he realised it was a possibility. It was not a pleasant thought, but who else could it have been? Realistically, it was worse to believe it was someone known to them who had killed Gabrielle.

CHAPTER TEN

'We have no proof and only one piece of circumstantial evidence, which certainly isn't going to satisfy the CPS. They'll laugh their bollocks off.'

'Succinctly put, Jack,' his chief inspector told him. 'That's why I want you to find the proof. I can't believe no one at that party saw anything odd or suspicious. And the victim didn't struggle, wasn't expecting to be toppled over that balcony, so it was someone she knew. Someone she trusted, more than likely.' He sighed. Like Jack he had hoped to have it neatly wrapped up by now. They knew all about the husband and his bit on the side, they knew what was in the will. They had also discovered that Mrs Milton may have intended altering that will, which left Dennis Milton firmly in the frame in view of his forthcoming redundancy. It had seemed perfect. Husband clobbers wife, inherits more than enough not to have to worry, then runs off with the bimbo. Better still, the bimbo's present, they'd planned it together.

But they wouldn't crack, neither of them, and he was beginning to feel Jack Pearce's theory was right. Only one little problem: the question of proof.

'Leave 'em long enough and someone'll make a mistake,' he told Jack. 'They're ringing each other up, visiting each other willy-nilly, there'll be a slip-up. Ease off on the pressure for a day or two. At least, let them think you have. Go on, shove off, you look tired.'

Jack was relieved. Initially he didn't think his superior had believed him. There was a way he thought he might be able to get that proof. It might be the only way. He didn't want to do it. It meant involving Rose Trevelyan.

'Shall I make a fresh pot?'

'No, thanks, Eileen, I must be going.' Maureen touched her sister's arm but there was no response. Eileen was staring at the seersucker tablecloth, trying not to cry.

'Come up for supper tonight.' Maureen didn't know what else she could say.

'No, I'll be fine. I'd better be here, in case he comes back. He'll want feeding.'

Eileen watched her sister leave and envied her her easy-going attitude. Jim had not been in touch for several days now and she did not know where he was staying. Pride prevented her from asking around.

It was a very odd thing, she reflected later, that it was on Doreen Clarke's shoulder she had finally cried when she turned up with a pot plant from Cyril's greenhouse to offer a bit of comfort.

Paul Milton and Anna were the next to be requestioned. Individually. They had both so far refused to say what their argument had been about. More people than Rose and Barry had noticed they were barely on speaking terms. Paul now insisted that it was nothing more than a disagreement, that Anna was wound up about the wedding. The detective constable made a note of this. Jack Pearce would be interested. From what he knew, no wedding date had been set at that point.

Anna claimed that whatever it was was so trivial she could no longer remember.

They, too, were allowed to leave.

When Rose heard Jack's voice on the end of the line she was pleased. She listened to what he had to say and was puzzled. 'I wouldn't ask if I didn't think it . . .' He had been about to say 'necessary'. 'It would be helpful. You're good at getting people chatting. Will you give it a go?'

'I suppose so. It shouldn't be difficult.'

'Good girl.'

Rose replaced the receiver. Good girl? How patronising. And no mention of seeing her again – apparently Jack Pearce simply wanted to use her. She would do as he wished, for her own satisfaction more than his. It was a very strange request he had made but he obviously had his reasons. And it had to be tomorrow.

She rang the Miltons' number. It was Dennis who answered.

'I hope I'm not being a nuisance—'

'Of course not,' Dennis interrupted.

'Only I'm doing some work on churches.' So far it was true. 'The thing is, I believe Gabrielle had some books on the history of Cornwall. I wondered if I might borrow one. You see, I thought I might try ancient monuments next.'

'Certainly. She would've been pleased to think you shared an interest.'

'Thank you. Would it be all right if I called in for them tomorrow? About three?'

The arrangement made, she hung up. Why Jack Pearce wanted her to borrow books she either already possessed or could get from the library was beyond her comprehension, but she had agreed to do it. Dennis would be fixing the car in the morning.

When the appointed time came Rose was shown into the lounge and Dennis asked if she wanted tea.

'No, I've just had some, thanks. I won't keep you, I feel I've taken up enough of your time.'

'No trouble. And there's no hurry to return them.' His face dropped as he realised they would no longer be needed. 'Ah, here's Paul. Paul, would you show Rose where your mother keeps her books?'

'I'd like to borrow a couple,' Rose explained.

'This way.' Paul preceded her up the curved staircase which ended in a gallery off which rooms ran. Rose had not been upstairs before. Paul opened one of the doors. 'This was Mum's studio.'

One wall was entirely of plate glass with a view over the garden and the sand dunes. There was nothing and no one to overlook the inhabitants.

The floor was wood block and there were two bright rugs. A couch was covered in tough cloth, pattered with zigzags in primary colours. There was also a table holding a sewing machine and an old wooden kitchen table. White walls were adorned with pieces of patchwork.

'Mum had several hobbies,' Paul said.

'It's a lovely room to work in.' It had a foreign feel, Mexican maybe. There was no sign the police had ever been in it but they must have searched everywhere thoroughly. Rose studied her surroundings, enjoying the smell of the new fabrics which covered the furniture but wishing she knew what she was doing there.

'Look. Mum did this.' Paul held out a cushion he had taken from a shelf. The cover consisted of many layers of material, slashed at random, letting the various colours show through, the edge of each gash neatened with minute stitches and, here and there, tiny beads, so small that Rose could not imagine a needle passing through them. But, more importantly, she was taking note of how

Paul spoke of his mother. There was regret and fondness in his voice as he showed her the almost completed piece of work.

'Would you like it?'

'What?' Rose's head jerked up.

'This. You might even finish it, there's only a corner to do.'

'Oh, Paul, I couldn't. I'd mess it up.'

'No, you won't. You paint, don't you? You must have a steady hand. Here, go on, take it.'

Rose did so. Of course she would love to possess it. She thanked him but wondered what Dennis would have to say about it.

'The books don't seem to be here, not the ones you wanted. They must be in the bedroom.'

Rose followed Paul across the landing. Gabrielle's bedroom was spacious and well furnished without being fussy. It was a room in which either sex could be comfortable. On the bedside table on the left of the bed were the two volumes Jack Pearce had asked her to borrow. Then he knew, Rose thought. He knew they were in here and guessed that no one would have removed them. But why? Unconsciously her head turned towards the tall windows which opened on to the balcony which ran around two sides of the house. Jack had wanted her to be in here, not in Gabrielle's study or workroom. She let Paul pick up the books and hand them to her, then they went back downstairs.

Dennis was on the phone so she smiled and waved and let herself out. The cushion and books she placed in a plastic bag she found under the dashboard. She saw many cars during the journey home but did not realise two of them held police officers.

Rose began seeing Paul in a different light but she suspected he was weak. Anna was the strong one, someone Paul could look to to tell him what to do, who would sort him out emotionally as long as the cheques kept coming in. What am I supposed to do now? she thought as she turned into her driveway. Did Jack expect her to ring him or would he be the one to make contact? She decided to leave it to him.

It had not crossed Doreen Clarke's mind that someone up at the house might be the murderer. It was Maureen who pointed it out to her over an afternoon cup of tea.

'Mr Milton? Don't be daft. He's too soft.'

'Paul then,' Maureen suggested.

Doreen shook her head. 'I'd know. You can always tell a killer by his eyes.' Not that I've ever seen one, she thought, but she'd know somehow or other. 'Besides, they've both spent hours with the police and they haven't been arrested.'

'There you are. They could be in it together. Dennis could have his bit on the side and they could share the money.'

Doreen had not meant to mention Maggie Anderson's name in relation to Dennis, but in the excitement it had come out. 'I don't know about that. I heard Paul asking his father for a loan the other day and Mr Milton said they couldn't do anything with the money until the probate was sorted out. I thought they'd have gone back to London by now, but they're all still there, the three of them. Madam expects me to wait on her hand and foot.'

Maureen smiled. She could imagine her friend's reaction to that. Doreen was quite capable of acting deaf or simply ignoring something if it was voiced as an order. 'Well, they seem to be taking long enough to find out who did it.'

'Yes, but think how many people were in the house that night.'

'Yes, plenty of suspects. Including you.'

'You're daft at times, you are. Still, you make a nice cup of tea.'

'Want another?'

'Please.' But Doreen's mind was elsewhere. She hoped Mrs Milton had not taken it upon herself to leave her anything in her will. With her and Cyril's present financial position, even a small amount might be considered as motive enough.

Routine had been so much disrupted lately that Rose went to answer the door without feeling in the least irritated. Dennis Milton stood on the step, the wind blowing his thinning hair across his scalp.

'They've arrested Paul,' he told her without preamble.

'Paul?' Rose tucked her hair behind her ears as if seeing him better would belie what he was saying.

'I don't know where else to turn. Anna's no good, she's shut herself in her room.'

'But I can't . . . I'm sorry. Come in.' The wind was whistling around the side of the house and there was a through-draught as the kitchen window was open.

Dennis was defeated, it showed in his face. In the kitchen she plugged in the kettle before thinking something stronger might be called for. Dennis accepted a small glass of whisky, and Rose poured herself a glass of wine. Underneath her concern for the man was an underlying feeling that people were dumping their burdens on her indiscriminately. She had to remind herself that it was her own interest which had encouraged it. And, if Paul was under arrest, Jack Pearce had beaten her to it. Her own feeble deductions were wrong. She could not see how her presence at the Milton house and that strange thing with the books had anything to do with it.

'What'll happen now?'

Dennis shrugged, his head bowed. 'I don't know. I'll get him a lawyer, I suppose, but he'll be lucky to get away with it.'

'Get away with it?'

'Oh, Rose! Surely you didn't think . . . ? No, no, it wasn't anything to do with his mother. Fraud. He was up to all sorts in London. God knows why he didn't come to me sooner. No, I do know.' He paused. He and Gabrielle had agreed after the last time they had bailed him out that they weren't doing him any good. 'I don't understand exactly what he's been up to but they'll be seeing his partner as well.'

Rose just stopped herself from saying she didn't believe Gareth was dishonest. She was not supposed to know him.

'As far as I can make out it's something to do with taking commission from property owners, showing them a signed lease then saying the lessee has backed out. Only eighty per cent of the commission's repayable.'

'But how can that happen? The people who sign can't just back out.'

'Quite. But it's worse than it seems.'

'Oh, no.' Rose realised what Dennis was saying, that it was Paul who had forged signatures on the agreements between his firm and the landlords, drawn up without the services of a solicitor.

'I'm afraid so. When questioned, Paul would give false details of the non-existent customer who obviously couldn't be traced.'

'You mustn't blame yourself, Dennis. You've done more than many parents would have.'

'I don't. It's Anna I blame. She puts so much pressure on him. Oh, I know that sounds as if I'm making excuses, but Paul's weak, he always has been. And he loves the girl – whatever she says goes.'

Rose had been right in her estimation of Paul's character. If he was that weak was it possible Anna had persuaded him to kill his mother?

'Another drink, Dennis?' She hoped she had said it in a tone which suggested she would prefer the answer to be no.

'I'd better not. I've got the car. I just hope that the engagement's off now. That would be one good thing to come out of it. I'm so sorry, Rose, to bring all my troubles to your doorstep. I wish I knew more people here.'

'You will, in time. If you decide to stay.'

Once he had gone Rose poured out a second glass of wine. I must eat, she thought. Later there would be more drinks with Laura; even if they decided to have a meal somewhere, Rose needed some food inside her first. A buttered roll filled with salad and corned beef took the edge off her hunger. This was followed by coffee, then a bath. Closing her eyes, Rose lay with suds damping the back of her hair as images of Jack Pearce, Paul, Dennis and Anna floated through her mind. And Jack's request. Was it of vital importance? What if he rang whilst she was out? And why did it matter so much?

Forget it, she told her reflection in the full-length mirror as she towelled herself dry. Turning sideways she thought, all in all, what she saw wasn't too bad. There was still a waist even if there was a little more padding on the hips than there once had been.

Because she had the hairdryer on its strongest setting, she did not hear the telephone ringing. When she went downstairs the light was flashing on the answering machine. The message was from Jack; he would try her again later. There was no clue as to whether the call was personal or not. Tempted to put Laura off, Rose decided against it. She was not about to make the mistake of losing a friend for the sake of a man. If it was that important Jack would keep trying until he got an answer.

The evening was not a success. Laura was not her normal vivacious self but rather withdrawn. Rose did not like to ask if it had anything to do with Trevor. Her own mind was preoccupied, too. So many ideas were jumbled and she was unable to concentrate on one thing at a time.

'Do you mind if we go now?' Laura asked at ten fifteen. They had walked as far as the Queen's Hotel on the front, had one drink there, then retraced their steps to Newlyn. It was a landing day, the harbour a mass of masts, the pubs reflecting the number of boats in by the persistent ringing of the tills. Mostly they enjoyed the noise and laughter but the two women needed solitude and a chance to think.

They parted outside the fish market, the shutters down now on the concrete building. 'I'll ring you tomorrow,' Rose said as she turned to make her way up the hill.

She had left a light on. The path was uneven and it was easier to see to fit her key in the lock. No danger of burglars tonight, she thought, seeing Jack Pearce's car outside, Jack himself at the wheel.

'Where have you been?' he asked as soon as she was parallel with his window.

'Out. Is it allowed?'

Jack got out of the car.

'I'm tired.'

'So am I. Did you get my message?'

Rose could not deny it. Had he looked, he would have been able to see through the front window that the message had been played back. The light was no longer flashing. Opening the kitchen door she realised he was right behind her. Without invitation he followed her inside.

'You've arrested Paul, then,' she said immediately, hoping to put him at a disadvantage.

'Not much escapes you, does it, Rose?'

'But not for the murder?'

'Dennis Milton's been sniffing around again, I take it.'

Rose resented his terminology but ignored it. 'I got the books. Had I known it was to be a wasted journey, I wouldn't have bothered. Did you just want to borrow them or something, and not like to ask yourself?'

'My, my. We are in a mood this evening.'

'Are we? I'm simply very tired.'

'Listen, it wasn't a wasted journey. I can't say more than that. I'll go now. I only wanted to make sure you did what I asked.'

'Do I get expenses?'

'Pardon?'

'Expenses. Petrol money? Loss of earnings? And I'll have to return them at some point.'

Jack's smile did not reach his eyes. Rose saw he

really was tired. The lines around them seemed to have deepened.

'Make sure you lock up,' he said before he left. 'Oh, I wondered if you were doing anything tomorrow evening?'

'I am, actually.'

'Barry Rowe?'

'I don't think that's any of your business, Inspector Pearce.' She smiled sweetly and shut the kitchen door before he could say anything else.

'Feisty little madam,' he muttered as he slammed the car door.

Rose heard nothing from Jack the next day. She did some housework and ironing before printing a dozen copies of the photograph the author had chosen from the contact sheet. There were two jobs in the diary for the following morning. After checking she had enough film and cleaning the camera lenses Rose sat down with a cup of coffee and a book. Her intention was to have a quiet evening alone, to simply relax and forget all that had happened. It was not to be.

'She what?' Anna was amazed that Rose Trevelyan had returned to the house on the pretext of borrowing some books. It was obvious what she was after. Dennis. Dennis would be a nice meal ticket for a single woman who had to work for a living. And Paul, the stupid fool, had encouraged it by giving her one of Gabrielle's bits of

202

sewing. And now Paul had been arrested. Of course, he would be released – he didn't have it in him to kill his mother.

Dennis, sick of Anna's attitude, had not bothered to tell her why he had been arrested. She had been out at the time, shopping in Truro.

Anna thought very carefully about what she must do. First, so as not to arouse suspicion, she must sit with Dennis and try to eat the meal Mrs Clarke provided. The woman, she thought, had no idea of sophisticated cooking. Dennis, she knew, would push the food around his plate. If she were Doreen Clarke she wouldn't bother.

'Do you want a divorce?' were the first words Eileen Penrose uttered when Jim returned for more clothes. She had seen him approach from the window.

'I haven't had time to think about it yet.'

'So I just sit here and wait for you to come to a decision?'

'It isn't easy. Not after all this time.' He was weakening, he knew that, but he did not want Eileen to know yet. They had been through a lot together and he had supposed that once the children left home his wife would relax, that her jealousy would become less of a problem. Living in a mate's back room was not his idea of a home life and Eileen could not be faulted on how she ran their home. But it was more than that – he loved her. Loved, not in love with, and Jim knew the difference. He saw her properly for the first time in years. She was too thin, eaten up by her anxieties, but she still had a nice smile. Not that she had smiled for ages. The expression in her eyes was not one he had noticed before, half pleading, half angry. She would not make the first move, of that much he was certain. 'Give me a few more days, love.' And with that he was gone.

Eileen did not move. He was coming back, she knew it. He had called her love.

The following evening he was back again, letting himself in with his key. He threw his bag into a corner. 'All right,' he said, 'we'll give it another go. But there's going to be some changes. For a start you're going to stop checking on my every movement. You could have got me locked up, you realise that, don't you?'

'I wouldn't have let that happen.'

Jim ignored her. 'And I won't be answering any of your endless questions from now on. If I want to take a drink, I'll do so. If I want to eat my supper in the pub, I'll do that too. And if you ever accuse me of going with another woman again then it will be a divorce. Do you understand that?'

'Yes,' Eileen said, turning her back so he would not see the gleam of triumph in her eyes.

But Jim was enjoying his own little triumph. For three of the nights he had been away he had shared the bed of Rita Chynoweth – and what made it even better was that, although he was sure no one knew, if the news did filter back to Eileen there was nothing she could do about it, not if she wanted him to stay.

Jim felt no guilt. For too many years he had been made to feel guilty over things he had not done. It was his own small revenge.

The gossip spread rapidly. Eileen was aware of halted conversations when she entered a shop and the nudges of women chatting on the pavement but she assumed they were discussing the split-up and Jim's return. Let them talk, she thought, head held high. The irony was that she had always believed him unfaithful when others hadn't and now the reverse was true.

DI Pearce had explained to the superintendent that the plan had not worked.

'I think you should give it another day, Jack,' he was told. 'After all, you can't guarantee the position's been made clear. We dare not take any risks now.'

Jack was glad to hear this. He was also glad to be operating from headquarters rather than from the Milton premises. He was never as comfortable on away ground.

Anna telephoned her office and said she would be back at work soon. Once the police realised Paul was innocent, he would be released. Meanwhile she had to make sure Dennis was not influenced by anything Mrs Trevelyan might say or do. Several times she had broached the subject of money with Dennis, playing on what she believed to have been Gabrielle's wishes, that she would have wanted Paul to be all right. Dennis had not said much but at least he had not given a refusal.

Anna was unaware that he was not even listening, that his thoughts were of Gabrielle and of the trouble his son was in.

Doreen Clarke was amazed when she learnt that Paul had been arrested. She, too, made the wrong assumption. 'To think I was under the same roof as a murderer, Cyril. I can't believe it. I could've had my throat cut any minute. And Cyril, I do wish you'd take that cap off when you're in the house.' She stirred a dollop of cream into the cauliflower soup she had made. Doreen believed a generous portion of the clotted variety every day never hurt anyone.

'Will you stay on?'

'Of course. No point in leaving now, when the danger's over.'

'There's a girlfriend, isn't there?' Cyril asked, finally removing his cap.

'Anna. Madam. God knows what she'll do now. They won't be engaged any longer, you mark my words. She tried to get round me this morning, she did. Came into the kitchen and tried to get me into conversation. She was asking about that nice Mrs Trevelyan. Rose, the artist.'

'Oh?' Cyril was studying the paper. It would not have taken much trying to get Doreen into conversation, he thought, but was wise enough not to say.

'I soon put her right. I said I was busy and that I wasn't going to discuss a friend of mine, especially one as nice as that. I told her, I said, "She's got a good head on her shoulders, she knows more than most around here." And then when she said she wanted some coffee I told her where the kettle was.'

Dennis and Anna sat in silence at the dining-room table and toyed with mushroom soup. Dennis had crumbled a bread roll but had not eaten any of it. He had arranged for a solicitor to be present while Paul was questioned but the man had told him not to be optimistic.

Chicken casserole and broccoli followed the soup. Anna ate most of it, not wishing to seem in a hurry to leave the house. Doreen nodded in satisfaction when she cleared the plates. It was a shame that Anna refused to eat cream, she looked as if she needed a few more pounds on her.

'I don't believe it.' Rose threw her book to one side and heaved herself out of the armchair. She was comfortable and pleasantly tired and well into the plot. Although she was tempted to let the answering machine do its job, she knew that would be daft. If she refused to answer the phone each time it only meant ringing back whoever had called. It was hardly an economical way of doing things.

'I thought you'd be out.' The surprise in Jack Pearce's voice was genuine.

'I changed my mind.'

He was thrown. He had planned a carefully worded message. Instead he said, 'Well, in that case, do you fancy meeting me for a drink later? There's a couple of things we need to discuss.' He paused. 'And I would like to see you again.'

How could she resist? 'All right,' she said. 'What time and where?'

'Eight thirty? I can't make it until then. Somewhere in town?' Normally he would have offered to pick her up but he did not want to compromise her as far as her neighbours were concerned. He named a pub. 'There's a chance I might be a few minutes late. It's unavoidable in this job. I hope you'll wait.'

'See you later.'

Jack was pleased. There was something he needed to tell her, which he could have done over the telephone, but he wanted to see her, to have her to himself on neutral ground. Last time they had got along fine.

There was time to finish the novel. Rose made another coffee and decided what, out of her limited wardrobe, she would wear. It was a mild evening but almost dark. The few remaining flowers took on different hues in the half-light and the grass was a bluish green where the fluorescent tube cast a paler rectangle on the lawn. Rose shut the back door but did not lock it.

Later she cleaned her teeth and changed into a sage-green pleated skirt and a cream blouse, then put on some make-up. She gathered her hair at the back and clipped it in place with a large wooden slide.

Downstairs she picked up her book to finish the last four pages before she set off for Penzance.

CHAPTER ELEVEN

Jack Pearce, fresh from the bath, was only running a few minutes late. He had, he realised, overdone the aftershave and rubbed off the surplus with a towel, wondering at the wisdom of taking Rose out. They were not teenagers, he could not buy her a couple of lagers or a few glasses of wine and leave it at that. Rose would expect more of him. Besides, he thought as he grinned at himself in the steamed-up mirror, she might easily out-drink me. For the first time in many years he studied his face. Was he good-looking? He did not know. He was used to what he saw, but what did Rose see?

Trousers, clean shirt and jacket, but no tie, that would be over-doing things . . . He checked his pocket for keys and wallet and left his flat.

Jack liked Rose – more than liked her – but just why, he wasn't sure. She was pleasing to look at and took no nonsense from anyone. She was talented and intelligent and moved around with the energy of someone half her age. But God help anyone who got her back up.

Since his wife, Marian, had departed, Jack had taken out several women but once the sexual attraction had waned they had bored him. They lacked something he needed by being too compliant or too obviously seeking a husband. Rose was interesting. There were depths to her he was sure he would never reach.

Jack whistled as he walked down the hill towards the sea. Lights from the salvage tug anchored in the bay rippled over the water and, to the west, a fishing boat chugged out of the harbour. It was a calm evening; the faint slap of water against pebbles was the only sound apart from an occasional passing car. Above the harbour the tiered lights of the houses of Newlyn twinkled. He paused and breathed in the air with its hint of kelp. An oyster-catcher called as it flew from the shore.

The Mount's Bay Inn was less than a hundred yards away. Rose would be sitting there, a drink in front of her. Jack anticipated her smile.

He pushed open the door. To his right, in the small dining area, a couple and a man on his own were eating. At the bar were three men, two of whom he knew. The window table was occupied by an elderly couple with a dog. There was no Rose. He ordered a drink and exchanged a few words with the solicitor at the bar, a prosecutor, with whom he had come into contact several times, then he sat down.

Rose used the pub, she would know the people present, but he could not bring himself to ask if she had been in. He was only fifteen minutes late. Surely she would have waited that long? He lit a cigarette. The obvious explanation was that he had told her he was likely to be late so she had not hurried herself.

Each time the door opened he glanced up expectantly. At nine fifteen, two pints later, he knew she wasn't coming.

'Similar?' the landlord asked when Jack placed his glass on the bar.

'No, thanks. I'm off now.'

He crossed the road and leant against the railing, staring at the sea, kidding himself that he was enjoying the view: hoping that Rose would appear, walking quickly from the direction of Newlyn. A youth cycled past him. Jack could not be bothered to challenge him – let him ride on the pavement if he wanted to.

'Sod her,' he said aloud, and started walking back towards the town. Not wishing to go home, he stopped at the London and began some serious drinking. Something stirred at the back of his slightly befuddled brain. He went to the telephone and dialled Rose's number. The answering machine came on. 'Rose,' he said. 'Rose, it's me. Jack. I'm in the London. I'll be here for another twenty minutes. Come in the car. I'll wait.'

He returned to the bar and ordered one more drink. If she did not arrive he'd get a cab and go over there. If

Rose didn't want to see him, fine. But he had to make sure she was all right. Maybe she hadn't stood him up. There might have been an accident, or perhaps some relation had been taken ill. Rose did not have his home telephone number and it was unlikely she would have tried to contact him at work. Her parents might have needed her. If she still had parents. There were so many things about her he didn't know.

After twenty minutes there was no sign of Rose. Jack rang for a taxi and was told one would be there in five minutes. He gave the driver the directions, feeling slightly ridiculous, like some love-struck youth hanging about for a glimpse of a girl. He knew the registration mark and make of Barry Rowe's car and dreaded seeing it outside the house.

'Just here. Hold on a minute.'

The driver pulled in, the engine running. Rose's house was higher than the road. Jack leant over. There was a light on in the front room but the curtains were drawn. No sign of Rowe's car. Then his stomach tightened. In the gap between Rose's Mini and the road was a car he recognised. Gabrielle Milton's car. It now belonged to Dennis.

'Back to Penzance, please. Drop me in Greenmarket.'

The driver shrugged, unconcerned at his passenger's strange request.

So that's the way it is, Jack thought. I should've seen it coming. Rose hadn't wasted any time. She had taken him for a fool. She might even have known Dennis before she met Gabrielle, might even have been having an affair with him. Why not? Dennis was no saint.

There were approximately thirty pubs in Penzance. If he couldn't get drunk tonight, he never would.

Rose had not heard the tap at the door. She was halfway down the stairs when she began to feel uneasy, to sense that she was not alone in the house. Laura would have called out. Whoever it was was not going to delay her – she was looking forward to the evening.

She pushed open the kitchen door. Anna stood leaning against the outer door, her hand behind her, still on the handle. 'I need to talk to you,' she said.

'Oh? You might have telephoned. I'm just on my way out. Perhaps you'd like to come back tomorrow.'

'I think we'd better get this over with right away.'

Rose hesitated. Anna's eyes were narrowed. Something was definitely troubling the girl. 'Five minutes then. In here.' She led the way into the sitting-room; it seemed more formal that way and Jack would probably be late. 'All right, what is it?'

'I want Gabrielle's books back, and I want you to stop asking so many questions about my future family. Why are you so interested?'

'Is that really any concern of yours?' Rose flushed, annoyed with herself for doing so. She had taken too much upon herself; she saw how it must appear from Anna's viewpoint.

'Is that any concern of mine?' She mimicked Rose. 'It

is, when it's blatantly clear you're after Dennis, that you want to take what's rightfully mine.'

'Yours? I don't understand.'

'Gabrielle promised she'd leave everything to Paul. Of course it would be mine as well.'

'But she didn't change her will.'

'She would have. Now it's Dennis's and you're after it.'

'Oh, Anna, honestly. I can't see what you're getting so excited about. I'm not after Dennis, as you put it.' She smiled to show how silly she thought Anna was being, yet underneath she was wary. The girl showed all the signs of being mentally unbalanced.

'Excited?' Anna swung round. Her coat flew open to reveal an expensive dress. 'You're trying to steal what's mine and you're going around like some bloody amateur detective attempting to put me in the wrong. You leave us alone, do you hear? Or I'll go to the police.'

And Jack would just love that, Rose thought. Her mind was working on two levels, coping with what was happening at the moment and analysing what she had previously suspected. As an intellectual exercise it had been one thing; this was something quite different.

I'll redecorate, she thought irrationally, once this is over – I really will. She was unaware that she was doing what she had done throughout David's illness, concentrating on trivia, not allowing her mind to accept reality.

'Why don't you sit down, Anna, and we'll discuss this sensibly.' Rose glanced at the carriage clock: the minutes were ticking away. How long would Jack wait before he rang or came to look for her? How long before he gave up and went home, the logical part of her brain said. She must keep Anna talking, defuse the situation if at all possible. Something else struck her: Anna was wearing gloves.

'There's nothing to discuss. You're a bitch, Rose Trevelyan.'

Even with the gloves Rose was astonished at the amount of pain the stinging blow to her face caused. She raised a hand and felt the heat. No one, she realised, had ever hit her before, not since the days of the school playground anyway. She had no idea how to react and could not bring herself to deliver a blow in return. 'As I said, I was on my way out. I'd like you to leave now. Or *I* shall call the police.'

'Do you know what you're doing, you stupid, stupid woman?'

Rose flinched at the fury in Anna's face. She was no longer attractive.

'You're stupid and crass and boring, living your parochial little life down here. As soon as a real man comes on the scene you're after him like a bitch on heat.'

Rose cursed herself for having become involved, for listening to Dennis in the first place and for not doing as Barry suggested, leaving it to the police.

'Did you hear me? You're a bitch.' Anna was screaming as she threw herself at Rose, her hands grabbing her hair, her arms strong from regular exercise.

Rose's eyes filled with tears from the pain. She pushed at Anna, realising her twenty years' seniority for the first time. All the times she had heard or read of ways of protecting yourself – kicking at a shin or poking fingers into an opponent's eyes – and still she could not bring herself to do it. She couldn't even scream.

Anna had backed her out of the room but Rose couldn't remember getting to the kitchen. The small of her back was against the sink, their faces were almost touching, and Anna's hands were around her throat. Rose had her hands on Anna's, trying to grasp the little fingers, to wrench them back and break them if necessary, because now she really knew the danger she was in. Anna had nothing to lose. The room was spinning. There was a harsh pain in her chest obliterating the other pain from the ridge of stainless steel cutting into her spine.

Anna's grip relaxed but one hand grabbed for her hair again. Rose knew, without doubt, that she had seen the bread-knife. If she got out of this Rose knew she would never leave dishes unwashed again.

Anna pulled back her arm. Fleetingly Rose was puzzled. Something dripped from the knife. Had she been stabbed and not felt it? She had heard that pain could be delayed. No, it was water, not her own blood.

Only then were all inhibitions gone. In a split second she acted instinctively, the need for survival an all-encompassing emotion. Had she really wished herself dead when David died?

Rose kicked out, hard, glad of the low-heeled

court shoes with their solid uppers. The blow hardly unbalanced Anna.

'No,' she shouted, and with every ounce of strength she possessed Rose bent sideways and grabbed Anna's wrist, kicking out again as she did so. She was free. In one movement she turned and picked up a kitchen chair.

Anna shrieked obscenities and raised the knife. Rose felt hot tears run down her face. 'No, oh please God, no,' she sobbed as she raised the chair and brought it down hard on Anna's head.

There was a sudden silence and then a strange noise. It took Rose several seconds to realise it was coming from herself. Her breathing was ragged and caught at her chest. Her whole body felt limp. She clutched at the table to steady herself.

Anna lay on the floor, her stockings and pants visible where her clothing had caught on something. Rose covered her. She was breathing. There was no blood. Rose knew that was bad, that gaping wounds and flowing blood always looked worse. It was internal injuries which were dangerous. What if Anna died? But what if she didn't do something quickly, if Anna revived, picked up the knife and plunged it into her before she had a second chance of defending herself?

Rose kicked the knife away, then picked it up and placed it in a drawer. In the sitting-room she picked up the telephone. 'Jack,' she said, 'come quickly, I need help.' The words sounded slurred to her own ears. There was no reply. She stared at the receiver wondering why she could only hear the dialling tone.

Shock, she thought, I'm in shock. Some normality returned. She punched out three nines with shaking hands, her index finger sliding off the last one. 'There's someone in my house. They're injured. I think they've killed someone.'

'Fire, police or ambulance?' the impersonal operator demanded.

It seemed an age until Rose was certain that they understood, that help was on the way. She wanted to stop them talking so they could get there faster.

She had to get out of the house. Her handbag was in the kitchen. Only afterwards did she realise how ridiculous it was to have felt she must have it with her, how many times people had endangered themselves for a few bits of paper and a couple of pounds.

Anna was stirring, trying to push herself to her knees. Her face was grey. Rose shoved her, knocking her to her side, then fled. She was halfway down the hill before she saw the blue light in the distance. She stopped then, and leant against the wall, unable to move. A breeze rustled the hedge behind her and she jumped but she did not have the strength to care if Anna had somehow caught her up. She sank to the ground, arms across her chest, head on her knees . . .

'Mrs Trevelyan?'

Rose looked up and saw the concerned expression on the face of a WPC.

'Come on.'

A blanket was wrapped around her and she was driven the short distance back to the house. 'I can't go in.'

'It's all right. You're safe now. The young lady's going to have a headache, but she's not badly injured.'

Rose allowed herself to be led inside and past the figure who was being attended to by another officer as they waited for the ambulance.

The next half hour was a blur. At some point Anna was taken away but the kitchen still seemed to be full of people. Rose sat at the table and drank the tea someone had made. Each time she raised the mug to her lips some spilt. There were spots on her skirt. The blanket was still around her shoulders.

Then the questioning began. Rose told them everything she knew and all she had done. At some point she thought she heard the telephone ringing but no one else seemed to notice so she might have been mistaken.

'Is there someone you'd like to stay with to night?'

'No. I have to stay here.' Rose knew that if she left, if she did not face what had happened, she might not want to return. She could not leave this house where she and David had been so happy.

'Someone who would stay with you, then?'

'Laura. No.' She shook her head. Trevor was home. They had enough on their plate already. 'Barry. Barry Rowe. He'll come.'

'What's his number, love?'

Rose stared at a man in plain clothes. How long had he been present? 'I don't know.' How many times had she dialled it? Yet she could not recall any of the digits. 'In my bag. My diary's in my bag.'

Someone handed it to her. She fumbled and pulled it out. There was more confusion but she ignored it. Then, it seemed seconds later, Barry was standing in the kitchen. 'Oh, Rosie, what have you been up to?' He put an arm around her and she started to cry. Long, gulping sobs that came from deep inside.

'Do her good,' a disembodied voice said. 'Delayed reaction. Can you stay the night, sir?'

'Yes. There's a second bedroom.' Even in such circumstances Barry was careful for her reputation. The police might have imagined they were lovers.

Not that night, nor at any other time, did Barry say, I told you so. He did not know the details of what had happened; in time Rose might tell him. What he did know, what he guessed from the number of police present, was that Gabrielle Milton's murderer had been caught.

Jack carried on drinking until closing time, the effect of those drinks beginning to tell. He was mellow. Past caring. In fact he was so far past caring that he might just walk over and tell Mrs Trevelyan exactly what he thought. No point in telephoning, she probably wouldn't answer when she heard his voice.

Not as steady on his feet as he believed himself to be, he reached Newlyn and lumbered up the hill. Something was wrong. He paused. There were no lights on in Rose's house, but that was to be expected, it was after midnight.

'Jesus Christ,' he muttered. Dennis Milton's car was no longer there. Parked in its place was the estate car Barry Rose drove.

Unable to believe the evidence of his own eyes, he began the walk home. Fortunately, he was unable to recall Rose's number and couldn't be bothered to look it up in the book or he would have left a less than pleasant message for her.

Instead, fully clothed, he got under the duvet and fell asleep.

'I'm sorry, Barry.' The spare bed had not been made up.

'It's OK. I was warm enough. Anywhere's warmer than my flat. It's not me we should be worrying about but you. How are you?' There was a slight air of embarrassment between them. It was the first time either of them had stayed in the other's house. Hotels in London didn't count. This was far more personal And Barry was flattered and relieved it was him Rose had turned to.

'Numb,' Rose replied. 'Bruised but otherwise numb. I suppose I look a mess.'

Barry smiled gently. 'I've seen you look better.'

Rose smiled back. Typical of Barry to be truthful.

'I'm going to make something to eat. Is there anything in the fridge?' He opened it. There were eggs and not much else. Scrambled eggs it would be then. He found bread for toast and made more coffee for Rose who, he noticed, was trembling.

'Barry? What about the shop?'

'Don't worry. I rang Clare before you were awake. She's opening up and she's prepared to stay all day if necessary.'

'No, I'll be fine.'

But she did not look it.

'There's a message on your machine, you know.'

Rose did not know. She had forgotten she thought she heard it ringing the previous evening. But she could not be bothered to see who it was. Not much seemed important any more. The smell of the bread warming under the grill filled the room. Rose was hungry. She thought she had never been so hungry and forced herself to eat slowly.

'I was right, Barry,' she finally said. 'I always believed it was Anna.'

And you nearly got yourself killed for it, Barry thought, but did not say. 'Do you want to talk about it?'

Rose shook her head. 'Not yet. Later maybe.'

When they had finished eating Barry washed up and dried his hands on the tea towel. 'Would you prefer me to leave?' he asked.

'Yes. I'm so tired. I can't thank you enough for being here.' She stood painfully and reached up to kiss him on the cheek. She did not see the expression of anguish on his face as he turned away, knowing that that was as much physical contact as he would ever receive from Rose.

'Take it easy. You know where I am if you want me,' was all he said before leaving.

'I'm going back to bed. The police're coming back later, I believe. I don't suppose I made much sense last night.'

'You're great, Rosie, you know that? And you'll be fine.'

Yes, she thought as she closed the door behind him, and locked it. I am and I will.

Two CID officers returned in the afternoon, one male, one female. Rose went over everything again, from her very first meeting with Gabrielle: this time in chronological order. She was still not sure why Anna had attacked her; she had not told Anna she suspected her, or anyone else for that matter. She was disappointed it was not Jack who was interviewing her but perhaps it was forbidden, like a professional/client relationship. There had been no telephone call either, apart from the one she had now played which was obviously left last night. Maybe he was off duty, unaware of what had happened, or he might think she had simply changed her mind and was too proud to inquire. Rose was wrong on both counts.

Alone once more she thought she had better eat. She had had nothing since breakfast. Pulling open cupboards she could not find anything she fancied, nor could she face going down to the Co-op or getting a takeaway. With a mug of tea in her hand she switched on the television for the local news. She was too exhausted to do much else and she was interested to see if there was any mention of Anna's arrest.

There was, but it was only a mention and no one was named.

A sound jolted her awake. On the screen was a half hour comedy programme. She had fallen asleep again. The sound was repeated. Someone was knocking at the door, but timidly. There were no lights on and she couldn't be seen from outside where she was sitting; she was tempted to ignore it. However, the flickering of the television may have given her away. If it was Dennis she would not ask him in, she could not cope with that man's problems tonight.

Turning down the sound on the set she went wearily to the door. Her body ached all over with a feeling akin to flu. Outlined through the frosted glass was a shape she did not recognise. Only when she opened the door did she see why. Jack Pearce stood holding an enormous bouquet wrapped in cellophane and tied with a bow.

'Hello,' he said tentatively.

'Hello.'

There was a pause of a few seconds. 'These are for you,' Jack told her, holding out the flowers. 'And this.' From the pocket of his jacket he pulled out a small box of chocolates awkwardly, the corner catching in the lining.

'Thank you.' Rose thought he looked worse than she must. His eyes were slightly bloodshot, his skin was sallow, and there was a slight stoop to his shoulders. 'You'd better come in.' She led the way to the kitchen. 'I'm sorry about last night. I was otherwise engaged.' She took the bouquet and began undoing it, averting her face as tears filled her eyes. There was no reason to cry but her GP, whom the police had called, had explained it was likely to happen for a day or two.

'I don't usually bring women flowers.'

He was ill at ease and Rose was pleased their roles were reversed. Did he feel guilty for not coming to make sure she was all right?

'How are you, Rose?'

'Recovering. Bruised and shaken, but otherwise all right. Jack?' Rose indicated the gifts. 'Why all this?'

'Guilty conscience.'

'Ah.'

'Because I doubted you, I thought certain things about you which I should have had the sense to know couldn't be true. I cursed you all evening. Then I got very drunk. I wanted to make it up to you.'

'It shows.'

'What does?'

'Your binge. You look dreadful.'

Jack laughed then. This was the Rose he had come to admire. 'Say no if you want, but are you up to going out? Nothing wild, just a quiet meal somewhere. I'll drive, I won't be doing much drinking.'

Rose did feel like going out. The tiredness had not worn off but she had spent the previous forty-eight hours under the same roof and had slept most of the day. A change is as good as a rest, she thought. 'Am I all right like this?' She indicated her jeans and thick jumper, under which was a shirt. She was still cold.

'You'll do.'

Rose trimmed the stems of the flowers and put them in a bucket of water. 'I must make a phone call first.' She went through to the sitting-room.

'Barry Rowe,' she explained a few minutes later. 'He was good enough to stay with me last night. He said he'd call in later to see how I am.'

Jack did not ask for further elucidation. He was in possession of the facts now. She need not know how he had misinterpreted them. Barry was her friend and she had had the decency to let him know she would be out rather than cause him anxiety or a wasted journey.

'I'm ready.'

Together they went out to the car. Rose felt the weakness in her legs after all those hours of lying down, but it would pass.

The restaurant Jack had chosen was expensive and, she noted, he had already reserved a table.

'I didn't do it with the assumption you'd accept,' he said, seeing her expression. 'It's just that it's popular and you need to book. I'd have cancelled if you said no.'

Seated, they ordered their food and some wine. Jack poured himself half a glass. Rose took a few sips and felt its effect at once.

'I always thought it was Anna,' she confessed. 'But I was wrong not to consider myself in danger. I might've caused you even more work. Jack, why did you want me to borrow those books?'

'We knew from Anna's background that she was

unstable and we also knew that people are inclined to tell you things they won't tell us. I knew the books were in the bedroom and I knew Anna considered you to be a nuisance, she believed you were moving in on Dennis Milton. I'd hoped she'd be at the house and take you up there herself, to the scene of the crime, as it were. I wanted your reaction to her own. I wanted you and Anna together in the room where Gabrielle was killed. Irrational, really, but I felt you'd, I don't know, sense something or get her to talk. If that failed I assumed Anna might well come to collect the books from you herself, to prevent Dennis doing so or you returning to his house. We, too, believed it was Anna, but how to prove it was the problem. She had free range of the house so fingerprints didn't count, and she often chatted to Gabrielle in the bedroom. We couldn't break her with our questioning but we thought if you could build up some sort of rapport with her, or, alternatively, if she hated you so much, she might say things she had not intended to say. We used you, Rose, I'm sorry, but you did seem to get yourself involved from the start.'

'Didn't you have her followed or put under surveillance or whatever you call it?'

'Yes. That's how help arrived for you so quickly.'

'What're you talking about? I had to ring the police myself.'

'I know.' Jack looked down and rearranged his cutlery. 'We had a man follow her to your house. He was parked outside. He saw Anna enter and waited. No lights were extinguished, there was nothing to show you were in any danger. Only when he heard someone scream did he radio in. People were already on their way before you rang.'

At the time, even when minutes and hours meant nothing, Rose had been surprised how quickly she was surrounded by people. 'He must have seen me, the man in the car.'

'He did. But he realised you were at least in a fit enough state to run. His concern was with the lady inside the house. He went in immediately.'

The starters were served. Rose dug her fork into the hot chicken liver salad and began to eat.

'I still don't understand it,' she said after several mouthfuls. 'This business with the will. Did she really kill Gabrielle for money?'

'Yes. Or at least, that's the obvious motive. There's more to it than that. No doubt the psychological reports will tell us. But she was a very mixed-up young woman. Always has been. She claims she was adopted, that she only found out when she was fifteen. Not true. Her natural parents are alive and well. She despised them for being ordinary, for not having money. It didn't help that she was considered to be beautiful, boys and men falling at her feet. It gave her inflated ideas of her worth.'

'It doesn't sound as if she needs a psychiatric report. You seem to have worked it out for yourself.'

'I can't claim that. Rose. We knew about the parents as soon as we began our investigations. They, and people her own age she used to know, told us. When she found out Paul's true financial state it sent her over the top.'

'But the will?'

'I was coming to that. From what she told us it seems she totally misconstrued what Mrs Milton said. They'd had a heart-to-heart. This took place soon after she became aware Paul was virtually broke. Anna went to Gabrielle to try to wheedle some money out of her, to keep Paul going. Gabrielle said that she wanted to do her best for Paul, that it was time she helped him properly, and that she had changed her will.'

'But she hadn't. Dennis implied . . .' Rose stopped. She, too, had misinterpreted things. Dennis had been surprised everything had been left to him. Of course, Gabrielle *had* changed her will, but in favour of Dennis, not against him as a punishment for his infidelity. And someone had told her that the Miltons were tired of bailing Paul out. Gabrielle, it seemed, had stuck to her word, had tried to make it possible for Paul to stand on his own feet. If he thought nothing was coming to him he would have to make much more of an effort. 'Maggie Anderson?' Rose continued. 'Did Gabrielle know of her existence?'

'We'll never know for certain.'

Rose leant back to allow the waiter to clear the plates. 'That was good. Very filling.'

'I hope you've still got room.'

'I have. I'd like to think she didn't know. That invitation, it wasn't Dennis's writing. Maggie would

231

have known that. She told me Gabrielle sent it, but the more I thought about it the more I felt that it was Anna who did.'

'Correct.' Jack raised his glass. 'It wasn't difficult finding out. The two women had shared the job of addressing them and sending them out a couple of weeks before the party. Anna took an extra one.'

'How did she know about Maggie?'

'Paul told her. He was worried his mother might get hurt. He'd seen his father and Miss Anderson in a restaurant somewhere or other. He confided in Anna, as anyone would their fiancée, just to get it off his chest, I suppose. We don't know how she found Maggie's address but maybe Paul told her the name – Dennis had no option but to introduce them at the time of their unfortunate encounter. He may even have said what she did – it would have been an excuse for their being together.'

'And Anna wanted her under Gabrielle's roof, to make sure she did find out, to show her she was doing the right thing by leaving everything to Paul.'

'Seems likely.'

'And she killed her because she found out otherwise?'

'Oh, no. It was far more cold-blooded than that. That would have been heat of the moment. She killed her because she couldn't wait for the money. Money which wasn't going to Paul anyway.'

'That's why she agreed to get married so quickly. She was sure Paul was about to inherit and she didn't want to give him a chance to change his mind.'

'That's about the sum of it. A lot of this is supposition at the moment but we've got a confession. Thank God.'

There was a pause as they both realised it might have cost Rose her life for them to be absolutely certain of having a case. Jack felt vaguely ashamed but he had believed Anna would say something to Rose, something which would give them a lead. He had had confidence in Rose's ability to make her talk.

Rose could hardly blame him. Had she not insisted on becoming involved, on dealing with matters she knew nothing about, Jack would not have come to her for the favour. The best thing was to try to forget it, to concentrate on the meal which had been placed before her.

'Damn it.'

'What is it?' Jack looked up, the pepper grinder in mid-air. 'I had appointments today. I forgot to cancel them. I'm not so affluent that I can lose business.'

'No need to worry. It's taken care of.'

'What?'

'Your friend. Barry. He cancelled them for you first thing.'

'He did what? How did he know?'

'Apparently your diary was lying on the kitchen table. He checked it.'

It had been, Rose realised. She had got it out to find his number the previous night. 'Hang on. How did you know he'd done so?'

'I called into the shop. Once I knew he'd been looking

after you, I asked if he thought you were up to going out tonight.'

'He knew?' So many things seemed to be going on around her, concerning her, yet she was not aware of them. Barry had not mentioned this when she rang him earlier. But, on second thoughts, he hadn't sounded very surprised either.

'He was kind enough to tell me to have a good time.'

Rose wasn't listening. 'Paul,'she said. 'How is he taking it?' He had lost his mother and his girlfriend in a very short time.

'At the moment he's denying it to himself. He relied on her for everything. Emotionally, that is. He was pleased to have someone to do things for. There was nothing he was able to do for his parents.'

'He could have tried harder, to get on without running to them for help.'

'Rose?'

She pushed the remaining pheasant to the side of her plate, too full to finish it. 'What is it?'

'Rose, promise me you won't do anything? I know you've a penchant for lame ducks, but let this be.'

'I will.' The last thing she wanted was to become embroiled with any more of the Miltons' problems. 'I wonder if it will bring them closer together? Dennis and Paul.'

Jack doubted it. The two men only seemed to have their grief in common. Once that passed – if it passed – things would revert to how they had been before.

'What's going to happen to Paul?'

'I'm not sure. It's not our case. The Met are dealing with it.'

'Will they take into account what's happened?'

'No. Paul was in trouble long before any of this. Can you manage a sweet?'

'No way. Not another thing.'

'You'd better knock back the wine, then I'll take you home. You look shattered.'

Poor Dennis, Rose thought when Jack went to ask for the bill. His wife dead, his son in prison, his son's future wife also locked up. What on earth would he do? Survive, that's what he'll do. She answered her own question. She had managed to survive.

'Jack? How did Anna know Gabrielle would die from that fall? I mean, she did push her over, didn't she?'

'Yes. But the PM showed that certain injuries were received before she hit the ground.' He lowered his eyes and Rose knew he would tell her no more. There were things that he could not reveal in case Anna changed her story, in case there was a trial after all, not just a hearing. Still, she couldn't help herself, couldn't leave it alone. 'But there would have been blood in the bedroom, surely?'

Jack grinned ruefully. 'There wasn't any when you dealt with Anna, Mrs Trevelyan.'

She felt the hot flush creep up her neck and decided it was time to keep quiet.

* * *

Rose cancelled her appointments for the next few days. She was still not up to working and, as people heard, one by one they were telephoning or coming to see her. Laura, tactfully, gave her a chance to recover but kept in touch by phone every day. Jack, too, rang daily.

At the end of the week he asked her out again.

'And whose car was that parked outside early this morning?' Laura asked when she called in for coffee on Saturday.

'You know perfectly well whose it was.'

'Well, how was it?'

'Pardon?'

'You know what I mean. What's he like in the sack?'

'None of your business.' But Rose was smiling, she did not need to tell Laura.

Laura was pleased. Rose had been without a man for far too long. Things were still not certain between her and Trevor but she had made an appointment to see the doctor. There might be something in this hormonal business after all.

'I'm not going to get the lurid details then?'

'No chance. It'd be all over Newlyn before lunchtime.'

'It's all over Newlyn already, my girl. Everyone knows a copper's car when they see one. And a lot of people know Jack. Don't forget—'

'Yes, I know. You all went to school together.'

'Seeing him again, are we?'

'Oh, bugger off, Laura, I've got things to do. I'll ring you tomorrow.'

Rose remained at the kitchen table. It had seemed natural, inviting Jack in for a nightcap and ending up in bed with him. She had felt a small pang this morning when she heard him swear as the shower attachment fell out of its holder, just as it had done when David was alive. The low ceilings of the house were fine for someone of Rose's dimensions, but there was nowhere to install a shower unit suitable for use by a tall man.

Jack was no replacement for David, she had known that from the start. They were different, and each attracted her for different reasons. And she had changed. Jack was like her now, there was always going to be a part of each of them that the other couldn't touch. For now she was content to take every day as it came.

He had not stayed for breakfast, not even for coffee. For that, too, Rose was grateful. It smacked of too much domesticity too soon. She had no illusions. There would be broken dates when work interceded, and the flowers and chocolates were a one-off. Jack was not a man to operate in that way.

Later, she got into the Mini and wondered why it wouldn't start. It seemed a lifetime ago she had asked Laura if Trevor would fix it. Laura, too, must have forgotten. She picked up the telephone to remedy the situation. Leaving the keys under the seat she strolled down to the sea and sat on a sandy bit of beach, her back resting against the high Promenade wall, the weak sun warming her face. She smiled at her indolence. Next week it was back to work.

Her parents, in their early seventies, were still full of life. They visited two or three times a year and, since David's death, had persuaded her to spend each Christmas with them, away from the memories. Rose knew that it was for her sake, that they did not enjoy the traditional celebrations. How nice to be able to tell them that this year she might have other plans. Either way, whether or not Jack was still around to accept her invitation, she was spending Christmas in Cornwall. She was not going to run away from possible pain again. They would make objections of course, but she knew they would sigh with relief when they put down the phone and rush off to book a cruise or a foreign holiday. They had the money to do so – why should she prevent them from enjoying whatever time they had left together?

Taking a paperback out of her bag Rose settled back to read, mentally waving two fingers at the still rumpled bed and the unpaid bills which would soon need attention.

Several small clouds drifted apart, exposing the whole of the sun. Herring-gulls paddled at the edge of the water, the tide far out. The salvage tug, which had been in the bay for weeks, had disappeared, maybe to refuel or maybe to be in on the kill. Rose felt a surge of optimism. David would understand her grieving days were over.